I0716654

*Jake Swan*

# GRANTREPRENEURS

GALLEON

*Grantrepreneurs*
© Jake Swan 2020
All rights reserved.

First Galleon Edition, August 2023
ISBN 978-1-7780-78170

Published by Galleon Books
Moncton, New Brunswick, Canada
www.galleonbooks.ca

Cover image and interior illustrations Adobe Stock.


*Grantrepreneurs* is a work of fiction. All characters and events herein – especially those based on real people – are entirely fictional. The author, for example, has never met Hulk Hogan, and has no idea if the WrestleMania VI champion owns a sailboat, visits Vancouver or hosts wild parties. All celebrity characters are fictional and do not in any way reflect the people upon whom the characters are based. The government programs discussed in this book are also fictitious. Due to its content, *Grantrepreneurs* should probably not be read by anyone thin-skinned and/or tone-deaf to satire.

Library and Archives Canada Cataloguing in Publication

Title: Grantrepreneurs / Jake Swan.
Names: Swan, Jake, author.
Description: Previously published in 2020.
Identifiers: Canadiana 20230477666 | ISBN 9781778078170 (softcover)
Subjects: LCGFT: Novels.
Classification: LCC PS8637.W363 G73 2023 | DDC C813/.6—dc23.

For Dad

I wrote *Grantrepreneurs* for my father while he was going through chemotherapy. Dad was an engineer, and spent most his life in the Canadian private sector. He had a terrific sense of humor, and never missed an opportunity to point out examples of extreme government stupidity and waste, though he always did so with a wry smile, seemingly half-annoyed with the wasteful expenditure of taxes, and half-impressed by the scheming rapscallions who had discovered new and innovative ways of exploiting the system.

I've written several unpublished books, some of which are probably better than *Grantrepreneurs*, but when he read this one, Dad said, "You have to publish it!" It was the only time he'd said that, so I promised I would try.

*Grantrepreneurs* is a work of humour. If it offends you, I'm sorry that you're taking life so seriously. Maybe try reading something inoffensive, such as "Studies in the History of Tax Law Vol 7." Or you know, try recreational drugs.

There are undoubtedly mistakes in this book. They are obviously mine alone, since there's no way in hell a Canadian agency, publisher or editor would touch this thing with a ten-foot pole.[1]

You can reach me at grantrepreneurs@outlook.com. If you are a lawyer writing to sue me, please keep in mind that my net-worth consists of a Chevrolet pickup truck and a massive student loan.

On a side note, I poke a lot of fun at Douglas Coupland, who happens to be one of my favourite authors. Everybody should read *Microserfs*, as it is among the finest books ever written and inspired this one.

Happy reading.

---

1	Publisher's note: We're obviously one-foot short of a full pole.

# 1

Tomato concentrate from ripe red tomatoes
Distilled vinegar
High fructose corn syrup
Corn syrup
Salt
Spice
Onion powder
Natural flavoring

*I ARRIVED IN VANCOUVER THIS MORNING.*

My plane landed at 3AM because my flight from the east coast had been grounded by fog. I was bone tired by the time I rolled out of the taxi, and it took me a few minutes fumbling with the keys that I'd received in the mail to figure out which was for the main door and which was for the apartment. At one point, I got what I now assume is the mailbox key stuck in the apartment door, and made a bit of a jangling racket trying to get it unstuck. Luckily, I didn't wake my new roommates. When I finally got settled, due to the time change, it was nine in the morning at home. This country is too big for the weary traveler.

I wasn't sure which bedroom was mine, so I laid my travel bag full of unfolded, but freshly laundered clothes on one end of the couch, and I placed my carry-on bag full of in-flight magazines on the other, and I laid across them using the carry-on as my pillow, and the bigger bag to elevate my swollen ankles. I don't know why I'm compelled to steal in-flight magazines. I feel like it might be my little way of sticking it to "the man" for the cramped seats. I'm a stiff-legged airline rebel, wreaking juvenile havoc through the friendly skies.

I awoke to the smell of coffee with a terrific crick in my neck. A young, handsome man (Michael, as it turned out) sat in the chair opposite me, and a young woman (Clara) sat Indian style on the floor at his feet. They sipped coffee from stained, chipped porcelain mugs and stared at me with what appeared to be clinical interest.

"Hey," I said, sitting up mechanically in a fashion that would cause no motion whatsoever through my sore neck. I moved like the Tin Man from *The Wizard of Oz*, only without the charisma.

"Hey, yourself," the young woman said.

"Are you here for Ray?" the handsome man asked.

"Ray?"

"I guess that's a no," he mused.

I offered my hand. "I'm Nick. I'm pretty sure I live here."

Neither of them moved. The young woman stared at the outstretched appendage, and hiked an eyebrow. I wondered if it was some kind of west coast thing. I took it back.

"Why are you on the couch… if you live here?"

I gestured to the walls around me. "I didn't know which room was mine, and didn't want to wake anyone up." They nodded, but said nothing.

"See, I took a job at Nova Health and they sent me this." I produced the keyring from my pocket.

They smiled, looking relieved.

The man got up and offered his hand then. "Sorry – we thought you were someone else. I'm Michael and this is Clara! There's been some confusion – there's this journalist – well, Ray says he isn't an actual working journalist anymore – he lost his job and he's apparently homeless, er – unhomed. I can't remember the lexicon we're supposed to use."

He looked to Clara.

"I think it's unhomed. I can't keep it straight," she said.

Michael nodded. "Right. It's apparently a pretty sad situation, at any rate."

"It sounds like it," I said.

"Anyway, let's forget about that for now. Welcome to Vancouver!"

As I eased myself from the cushions, Clara got to her feet in one fluid, springy motion. She reached out to shake my hand. Her grip felt firm and warm, and her skin had the youthful elasticity mine would never recover. Michael's had been the same.

I realized I was probably ten years their senior, and I felt a jolt of apprehension, thinking I'd perhaps accidentally taken a job meant for graduate-level college kids.

Clara and Michael both wore tight-fitting workout clothes and were obviously very fit. I was instantly aware of my flabby frumpiness.

"You look stiff," Clara said, as I tried to stretch my back, "kind of like the Tin Man, from *The Wizard of Oz*."

"But with less charisma," Michael finished.

"It's true," I agreed; "I'm uncharismatic."

Clara's rich, auburn hair and perfect teeth spoke of youth, and health, and, if I'm being honest with myself, what I guessed was a good deal of money. Straight, perfectly white teeth don't come cheap. My own are crooked, and stained.

I made a mental note not to smile too widely. I would hate to be judged on day-one for my ugly maw.

Beyond their appearance, both Clara and Michael radiated a bright, hopefulness that had long-ago been kicked out of yours truly. Their faces were kind, and eager, and full of potential.

I self-consciously rubbed my hand over my own haggard countenance, uselessly trying to smooth away the graven crow's feet at the corners of my eyes.

Yawning away the last vestiges of sleep, it occurred to me that I'd just been confused for a vagrant.

"Do I really look homeless? I mean… uh… unhomed?"

"Well, you look weary," Clara said. "Weariness and destitution are easy to confuse. I hope we didn't offend you."

"Not at all."

"It's particularly tough to tell when someone's sleeping," Michael added. "Especially on bench-shaped furniture."

I gestured at their gym clothes "Are you guys going running?"

"We were going to, but it's raining buckets," Clara said.

"Well, that, and we saw you on the couch," Michael added, "we thought we should investigate."

Clara showed me to my room. I noticed how nice she smelled as I trailed behind her. Here it was, first thing in the morning, she presumably had yet to shower, and yet she smelled like lilacs and juniper. I wondered if I might be too shabby to be roommates with these somewhat fabulous people.

She opened the door, then stepped back and motioned me in with her arm, the way Bob Barker used to motion a *Price is Right* contestant towards the big spinning glitter-money wheel. The room was small and dark, but seemed clean. The mattress on the twin bed was worn and sagging and reminded me of college. The bed had no sheets, and I made a mental note to buy some. The sole window was inexplicably covered with butcher paper. A Post-It note was stuck to the butcher paper. I squinted.

"Do Not Remove Butcher Paper."

I noted a sliding door on the near wall and assumed it was a closet, but there was another Post-It note.

"Do not open sliding door."

"What's with this?" I asked.

"It goes to the bathroom," Clara said. "We use the door from the hallway. Best just to pretend this one doesn't exist."

"And the paper over the window?" I asked.

"We don't know," she said. "Nobody's been in this room since any of us moved in."

"So you just left it papered over?"

"It seemed like the right thing to do," she said, "given the instructions on the note."

She walked back to the hallway, gently closing the door behind her.

There was a small desk in the corner, and I set up my laptop. I found a Wi-Fi channel labeled "APT405." I went back to the living room and asked Michael for the code.

"It's on the router," he said and showed me the twenty-character string of alphanumeric gibberish that had been written in magic marker on the blue plastic. I took a photo of it with my phone, but it still took me three tries to log in, because there were two zero's and one O. Then I entered it again on my phone and my tablet, and each time I did, it took me three times to remember which were O's and which were zeroes. Nine attempts in total. Personal observation here – using zeros and O's in your router password should be punishable by dismemberment.

I didn't have any new emails.

•

After showering and dressing, I went back to the kitchen to make myself a coffee, and another man – Ray, I assumed – leaned against the kitchen island, spreading peanut butter on toast. He got some peanut butter from the edge of the jar on his hand and licked it off, then seemed to notice me and smiled.

"You must be Nick," he said, saluting instead of offering the recently licked mitt. "Glad you made it out. I heard you were fogged-in. I'm surprised to see you up so early."

Ray's voice had a hint of gruffness that betrayed an inner wisdom defying his young age. He wore a loose-fitting Bass Pro t-shirt and jeans, and had short-cropped blond hair and ropey muscles. He was not particularly "west coast," in style or presentation.

"You're from New Brunswick, right?" he asked.

I nodded, and started to pour myself a coffee from the carafe.

"Don't drink that shit," he said. He actually reached out and took the cup from my hand, and put it back in the cupboard. "Don't get me wrong, Michael's a swell guy, but whatever colon-cleansing additive he puts in that coffee must have been born in the depths of hell, itself. I tried it once, last week. Let me just say this – I'm grateful to have any internal organs left."

"But it looked like they were going for a run – he and Clara. Surely they wouldn't..."

"I think they must stop for a shit at the public restroom along the sea wall. As far as I can tell, Clara hasn't had a dump in the apartment since she got here." He shrugged. "Some people are like that."

"And Michael?" I asked.

"Michael too," Ray said. "It's kind of incredible. I mean, I'm not keeping close tabs on the situation or anything, so who knows if there was an odd crapping here or there, but it certainly isn't a regular thing. To get two of them like that? What are the odds? On the plus side, I suppose it means more toilet paper for you and me."

Ray led me to the staircase and we hustled out of the building and across the street to JJ Bean Coffee. There were expensive sports cars parked everywhere along the curb. Even though it was early and it was raining, you could hear their racing engines echoing off the glass-walled towers around us.

"Have you been to Vancouver before?" Ray asked.

"A long time ago," I said.

"See these stickers?" He pointed to a yellow "N" in the rear windshield of a lime-green Lamborghini parked by the coffee shop. "That means novice. When you see these on Ferrari's and Porsche's and Lamborghinis, look the fuck out. Take a step back from the curb."

"OK..."

As if to make his point, the light at the bottom of the hill changed and a fire-engine-red Ferrari screamed up the road past us, its tires struggling to find purchase on the wet asphalt. I caught a brief glimpse of what appeared to be a ten-year-old Asian boy behind the wheel. Ray instinctively shot his arm out and muscled me six inches further back from the road. The car went by so fast I didn't notice if it had a yellow sticker.

Ray shook his head, clearly genuinely distressed. "Someone's going to get squished."

I held the door for him at the coffee shop, where Ray paid for my latte. He then ordered a black coffee, and I felt a little guilty since my drink had cost a lot more.

We sat at a table by the window, and I noticed all the other patrons had MacBooks open and they all clicked away at their keyboards.

"Everybody's working early," I said, to make conversation.

"Not working," Ray said; "they're writing."

"How do you know?" I asked.

"Look at their shoes."

I did as he instructed. A few seconds passed. "What am I looking for?"

"You know about sneakers?"

"Shoes for sporting occasions."

"More like status symbols. Yesterday's S-class is today's Air Jordans."

He pointed to a pair of red sneakers attached to a middle-aged Asian man who typed fastidiously away at his MacBook. "Now look at those."

"Yes…"

"Those are the Nike Air-Yeezy," he said. "Twelve thousand dollars a pair."

"You don't say."

"And over there – you see those?" He indicated a pair of bright-white sneakers with gold accents. The gorgeous Middle Eastern woman wearing them noticed us staring, and rolled her ankles to show off the sneakers in side profile. She smiled as she did so, modeling the footwear for our benefit.

Ray lowered his voice a little. "Air Jordan 12's. And yeah, they're men's sneakers and they're too big for her, but that isn't the point. The point is, they're about five-grand."

"OK," I said, "but how do the sneakers tie in with the writing?"

"All these people are in the leisure class. I know that because these sneakers are so rare and hard to find, that finding them becomes a full-time pursuit. They already own everything else they want, so they get into sneakers."

"Right, but why are they *writing?*"

"Because most writing grants aren't tested against your net worth. Some of them think they're the next Mordecai Richler. Some of them just do it for the social side – to meet other people who made millions in real estate or whatever. It's one of the things rich people do around here."

"Surely they don't need the grants if they're worth millions."

Ray laughed. "Need has nothing to do with it. Think of it more like a contest called 'Who can get the most government money.' They're very competitive with one another about it. They use the grant money for the sneakers. It's kind of their way of showing off."

"And they all spend all day writing at JJ Bean?"

"Oh, no, not just JJ Bean. They're everywhere. Every artisanal-quality coffee shop in Vancouver is the same. And they don't spend all day – they usually put in an hour or so every morning. Just enough to keep their grant. It's really quite a thing."

"Are they any good?"

"In general, no. But they're good at getting grants. Or at finding the people who can get them the grants."

I shouldn't have cared, but I couldn't help but bristle a little.

"Why doesn't the government crack down? If they aren't producing anything, I mean, they..."

"Listen, Nick," he cut me off, "there are layers upon layers of government employees, with the sole purpose of getting these grants out there. Now, when your standard offshore multimillionaire files a tax return, his or her accountant can type 'Writer,' in the blank for employment. That makes the government happy because they want these people to stay and spend their money here. And the grant people are happy because they've successfully given out a grant. The writers are happy because they've got sneaker money. Everyone's happy. Do you follow?"

"I guess," I said, "but don't the grant-awarding agencies expect some kind of output in return?"

"Just enough to pass an audit."

"Well, what about real writers?"

"Think about it. When was the last time you heard a big success story about someone who started with a government grant? The grant industry is its own self-contained economy! The message is the medium, and all that."

"So, you're saying the system works?"

"It doesn't just work! It thrives! It's our bread and butter so to speak."

"OK." I wasn't really sure it was OK. But I said it because I didn't want to get off on the wrong foot, and also, because Ray had not only paid for my beverage, but had saved me from accidentally drinking an unknown laxative, all within the past fifteen minutes, and I figured he deserved the benefit of the doubt.

"There is one small problem, though," he leaned in close, and half whispered. "There's this journalist. Well – a homeless guy who thinks he's a journalist. He used to work for the Fraser Institute, so I'm guessing he used to be some kind of economist. Apparently, he had a mental breakdown and ended up on the streets. I got a call last week from one of my former business partners that he's looking to do some kind of exposé piece about government grants, and publish it on his blog."

"The homeless guy has a blog?" I asked.

"Everyone has a blog," he said. "A blog or a vlog. Get with the times, dude."

"Right," I said. "Sorry."

"Anyway, it's important that this guy doesn't learn just enough to be dangerous, and somehow blow up the whole ecosystem. His name is Frances McCain, so if he approaches you, it's probably best not to engage him. We have a pretty good thing going. We don't want to screw with it."

"Got it," I said. "If a homeless economist-slash-journalist approaches, turn the other way."

"Right," he said. "But make sure he isn't a homeless accountant."

"Accountant?"

"The homeless accountant is a friend of mine."

"Got it," I said. "Economist bad, accountant good."

"Perfect," Ray said.

I glanced at his shoes. He wore Nike sneakers with a tropical pattern material and a bright orange swoosh. He saw me looking. "Lebron 9's," he said. "Seven grand."

"So why is the homeless economist looking for you?" I asked.

He fished out his wallet and handed me a creased business card.

**Ray Butler**
**Grant Connections**
**1 604 331 3603**

"I thought you worked for Nova-Health," I said.

"I do — well, actually, we changed the name last week to A.I. Plus Womxn's Health Solutions. That's with an $x$ instead of an $e$. You know, inclusivity and shit. Anyway, you're probably going to have to redo your employment contract."

"Wait, what?" I stammered. "Why the name change?"

He nodded towards the card. "Why do you think?"

"OK," I said slowly. "Do you still work for Grant Connections too? Are you, like, a consultant or something?"

"No, I sold Grant Connections. Made out pretty well too, I must say. Hence the shoes."

"Who bought your business?"

"The federal government. They paid a mint!"

"I'm a little overwhelmed," I admitted. "All these people," I gestured around the room, "they're independently wealthy and getting grant money from taxes being paid by people who work for a living, and they do it just for the thrill of it?"

"Essentially, yes."

"And the government who gives out these grants bought your business, which is designed to help people exploit grants?"

"That's about the long and the short of it."

"That's kind of messed up," I said.

Ray looked disappointed. "Is it any more messed up than repaving highways that don't need repaving? Or building infrastructure for a shrinking society out in New Brunswick, where you woke up yesterday morning?"

"I suppose not."

"It's the way of the world," Ray explained. "And it netted me some pretty sweet sneakers."


The rain let up by lunchtime so I decided to walk to Costco and buy bed sheets and pillows. I was concerned that it might rain again on the way home, so I added an umbrella to my shopping list.

Michael joined me, explaining that he wanted to buy a Costco-sized jar of Matt and Steve's Extreme Beans, Garlic and Dill.

"That's it? Anything else?" I asked, as we queued for the register.

"I'm condimenting," he said.

"Condimenting what?" I asked.

"It's an experimental diet," he said. "I'm writing a book."

"You only eat condiments?"

"I've lost fourteen pounds. I get all the sugar and fat I want, so long as it's in condiment form."

"But I saw you having a coffee this morning," I said.

"That was just Bulletproof Coffee Oil additive and cream. Condiments only, Nick. You should try it." He looked at my belly. "I bet I could strip twenty pounds off you in no time."

"Maybe," I said.

It started to drizzle as we walked back to Yaletown. "Oh man, I forgot the umbrella," I said.

"No problem," Michael said, looking around. "Here – hold my beans."

I held the reusable fabric bag that carried his jar of extreme beans. The bag had a picture of a sea turtle on it. I thought it was embarrassingly virtuous. My pillows and blankets and bread were in my carry-on backpack-style bag, but if Costco used plastic bags, I would have taken them.

Michael turned off the footpath, and strode to the rear lot of a condominium complex. I followed a dozen or so steps behind.

He approached a set of dumpsters, and to my surprise, he opened the lid of the largest of the industrial green receptacles, before climbing up and over. A moment later he emerged with two compact umbrellas. He popped one over his head and danced back to me, looking very much like Dick Van Dyke. He handed me the other.

"How did you know..."

"It rained this morning," he said. "When it stops raining, everyone just chucks their umbrella in the nearest dumpster instead of carrying it everywhere. Vancouver is a walking society – people are acutely aware of the risk the internal combustion engine poses to the global climate. But they don't seem to consider the landfill-related consequences of wasteful umbrella management practices. It's quite fascinating."

He paused while I opened my umbrella.

"Did I tell you I used to be a freegan?" he asked.

"No," I said.

"It was wonderful," he explained. "I didn't pay for food for two years. I ate leftovers – mostly out of the dumpsters behind restaurants. I saved a fortune. It's how I found out about the umbrella tossing thing."

"Why did you quit?" I asked.

"I got food poisoning from some bad shrimp behind ToJo. After that, it just seemed kind of foolish to take the risk."

"You ate shrimp out of the trash?"

"I used to all the time. But then I got sick – and around that time I made a bundle of money off a few houses in North Van. So, I decided to try condimenting to lose the weight I'd put on from the freegan diet. And well, here we are."

"Wait though. If you and Ray have all this money, how come you're living in a group condo?" I asked.

"Well, for one, it's cost effective since the company pays the bills. Just because we're rich, doesn't make us stupid. And two, because this is a lonely city, and it's nice to get to know people."

"You're an interesting guy, Michael."

"Have you talked with Clara yet?" he asked. "Now she's interesting."

As it turned out, Clara was gone by the time we got back to the apartment. She left a Post-It note on the kitchen counter that said "I'm sailing with Peter Mansbridge and Hulk Hogan. Don't wait up."

I was tired but I knew it would be a bad idea to go to bed and screw up my sleep cycle even worse, so I went to the grocery store for a salad, a loaf of bread and a case of Diet Coke, and then stopped at the Yaletown wine store for a bottle of BC red. While I was at the wine store, my mother called.

"Oh hi dear," she said. "Could you come over to see your

brother? He stepped on a nail and I'm worried about tetanus."

"Mom, I'm in Vancouver," I said. "I moved here yesterday."

"Oh doesn't that just top it off," she said and hung up. Mom had driven me to the airport. I called her back.

"Mom – why is Jeff there?"

"He wanted to come see me. Is that so hard to believe? He came home for a visit, and I asked him to put the barbecue out for me, and he stepped on a nail. It went right through his foot."

"Like Jesus?" I asked.

"Don't be blasphemous, Nicholas. Jesus has done a lot for our family."

"Sorry, Mom."

"Anyway the nail went through his foot and I was hoping you would come over and take the nail out and put iodine in the hole for him."

"The nail is still in his foot?"

"It's attached his foot to your father's old Ugg boot. It's really quite a mess."

"Take him to the hospital, Mom," I said.

"We'll be waiting for hours!".

"Leave him there – you don't have to wait."

"That's not fair to Jeff," she said. "He's had a very rough go of it. He quit his job last week."

"Mom. You're going to have to take him to the hospital. He can't go through life with his foot nailed to an Australian slipper. He'll get an infection."

"Why did you have to go off to Vancouver, just as Jeff was coming home?"

Before I could answer, she'd hung up again.


When I got back to the apartment there was a second note beside Clara's original Post-it. It read, "On rooftop drinking wine."

I climbed the stairs to the rooftop patio. I carried a bottle of wine and a small stack of red plastic event-cups I'd found in the cupboard. I wrestled with the keys to open the rooftop door and almost dropped the bottle in the process. The door opened into a narrow outdoor corridor constructed of vine-bearing trelliswork. A rock pigeon landed on a bare spot on the wood. I wondered if someone was bird-keeping on the rooftop like in all the movies I'd seen about people who live in big city apartment buildings. The pigeon stared at me for a moment. A soft *crack* emanated from somewhere behind the stairwell enclosure, and a small burst of feathers puffed out of the bird's breast, and floated away with the breeze. The animal fell stone dead on the patio-brick walkway. I heard Ray, from around the corner, say "Sweet!"

I peeked around the brick wall enclosing the stairwell, to find Ray and Michael sitting on patio chairs. Ray was busy, loading a pellet into a break-barrel air rifle.

"Hold your fire," I said.

"Nicholas!" Michael exclaimed. "Have some wine!" He tilted a long-stemmed wine glass full of brown liquid in my direction.

"I thought you were condimenting!" I called across the patio.

"I only drink popular cooking wines and sherry," he said. "It counts."

I made my way over, stepping over another dead bird. "What's going on, guys?" I asked.

Ray sighted in on another pigeon and shot it dead.

"Nice shootin', Tex," Michael said, before turning to me to explain. "Ray here has an extermination contract with the building manager. Ten dollars a pigeon!"

"They were shitting all over the AC units and luxury vehicles parked at the curb. Something had to be done," Ray explained.

"How many have you got so far?"

"What, tonight?"

"Sure."

"Sixteen." He took aim at something on the other side of the rooftop and fired. "Make that seventeen."

"So you made one hundred and seventy dollars by shooting pigeons tonight?" I asked.

"Yeah – so far. But the night is young. The pigeons see the dead birds and they can't tell they're dead. They think it's a pigeon party. Pigeons are idiots."

"How much are you making?"

"On average – I'd say about three hundred dollars a night."

"Wow," I said, taking the bottle of wine from the table between Michael and Ray. I left Michael's cooking sherry where it sat.

I poured some Malbec in a plastic cup. "I didn't know extermination was so profitable."

"Oh it can be – especially in a real estate bubble, when the difference in valuation between a building with a pigeon problem and one without a pigeon problem is in the tens of millions of dollars."

I felt a little silly using the plastic cup. Even though I was older than the other two, it seemed kind of college-grade. I also noticed that Ray's wine was much nicer than the one I'd brought. Having said that, I wasn't the one with the pellet gun.

I swiped the moisture off a plastic deck chair using the side of my hand and took a seat. "There's not much wind this evening," I said. "I wonder how the sailing is going."

"My guess," Michael said, "is that they're just having a party on Hulk Hogan's boat in English Harbor."

"That seems like such a random thing," I said.

"Sometimes Vancouver can go sort of non-linear," Ray explained. "I think it has something to do with money."

"It used to bother me," Michael admitted. "I used to feel like I needed a break every once in a while, and I'd fly to Kingston or Hamilton or Windsor for a week, where everything was normal. I would sit in a Holiday Inn Express hotel room and watch pay-per-view like a normal person just to decompress, and then I would fly back home. But once you come to terms with it, and start to go with the flow, you realize that normal can be kind of boring.”

“Back in New Brunswick, how much TV did you watch?” Ray asked me.

“Probably an hour or so before bed.”

“How much do you think you’ll watch here?” he asked.

“Don’t blow my mind – I’m too jet lagged for that, today,” I said.

“My point is, you’ll watch less because you’ll feel less of a need to live vicariously through other people’s stories. At least that’s what it’s like for me. When I’m here, I kind of feel like I’m part of a story myself, almost all the time.”

He lined the pellet gun up on a bird and shot it off the trelliswork. “Eighteen,” he said.

While we sat there chatting and shooting pigeons, I learned some things about my new roommates. To save time I have compiled them into a Buzzfeed-style list of attributes.

### Michael

— Born in North Vancouver.

— Most often checked iPhone app – Tinder.

— Possibly bisexual – his words, not mine.

— Used to work in real estate.

— Was once held at gunpoint during a house showing by a Chinese mobster named Wu Chung. As it turned out the house had belonged one of Wu Chung’s henchmen, who had broken his neck in Hong Kong during a figure skating competition. While Wu held a gun on Michael, another of his henchmen searched the house for five kilograms of missing heroin, which, as it turned out, had been stashed in dry-spaces in the false-bottoms of the vases that held the decorative potted ferns. During the ordeal, Michael and Wu became fast friends, and now they hang out most weekends.

— I realize that last point was not point form but I think it deserved some fleshing out.

— Likes dogs.

**Ray**

— Born in Saskatoon.

— Most often checked iPhone app – Liftoff Capital.

— Worked in software (whatever that means.)

— Has sold three companies, including Grant Connections, for an undisclosed sum.

— Is unable to turn down a paying job or an opportunity to save money.

— Believes this is because the only time he saw his father cry was when the old man explained that he hadn't saved enough money to send Ray to college.

— Once pulled someone from a burning vehicle after cutting their seatbelt with a pocketknife.

— Always carries a pocketknife.

— Considered pulling someone from the vehicle a typical act of Vancouver randomness, and nearly forgot about it until it drew national media attention when the person pulled from the fiery wreck turned out to be *Grey's Anatomy* heartthrob, Patrick Dempsey.

— Was invited to be a guest on *Ellen*, but declined as he was unable to break a pre-existing engagement.

— The prior engagement was a one of a series of well-paying deals Ray had with a corrupt real estate agent, who, in trying to dissuade a couple from buying a reasonably priced condominium, hired Ray to sprinkle seafood restaurant waste around the balcony and parking lot in order to create a "stench" and to portray the building as having "a seagull problem."

— Subsequently, Ray was contracted by the building owner to take care of the seagull problem.

— He also purchased the condominium unit at a steeply discounted price, and sold it two weeks later for an enormous profit.

— He describes the experience as "lucrative."

— Likes dogs, but only if they are working dogs.

— When asked if he means guide dogs, he states, "I wish I had a dog to pick up these fucking pigeon carcasses for me."

After a while, Michael found a love connection on Tinder, and Ray and I decided to call it a night. Tomorrow is the grand opening of A.I. Plus Womxn's Health Solutions. I'm uncertain what to expect.

Back in my room, I couldn't sleep. Being something of a country-mouse, I'm not used to city sounds so close to my window. I decided to start writing this journal. I will try to update it as things develop.

# 2

Aged cayenne red peppers
Distilled vinegar
Water
Salt
Garlic powder


*I MET THE PRIME MINISTER TODAY.*

I don't want to put the cart before the horse, but there you go. I'm beginning to understand what Ray meant when he described Vancouver's tendency to go "nonlinear."

But let's go back and look at the day anyway because Prime Minister or not, it was our first day at A.I. Plus Womxn's Health Solutions.

I woke up early, still jet-lagged, and went for a walk along the seawall. I admired the harbor and the boats, the stillness of the morning. I saw a few people running, but most of Vancouver seems like it's on Toronto time. I suppose the stillness of the morning pulled me into a sense of false punctuality, and before I knew it, I was on a beach with a giant, rust-colored hulk of a sculpture that I suppose was meant to resemble whale ribs, and when I checked my watch, I 'd walked almost an hour. I had to rush back to the apartment. I broke a sweat, but realized I didn't have time to shower before my first day at the new job. It was embarrassing.

Everyone at the apartment had been waiting for me. Ray looked quite proper in a shirt and tie over jeans. Clara was more millennial, wearing a scarf over a Ramone's T-shirt and blazer. Michael looked chic in skinny jeans and a slim-fit paisley shirt.

I shooed them out the door before quickly throwing on a rumpled sports coat, an XL blue denim shirt and some gap khakis. I caught up to them waiting for the Canada Line train. The air was humid, and I could already feel sweat seeping through the material of my shirt.

A.I. Plus Womxn's Health Solutions is based in a modern, cube-shaped turquoise glass building on Cambie Street. We couldn't get anywhere near it.

News vans lined the streets and a plywood stage had been erected on the sidewalk outside the front door. Hundreds of people milled about, spilling onto the street. Among them, dozens of Arab men and women (in burkas), quite a few Asian folks, who spoke loudly to one another in Mandarin, and people with crutches, people in wheelchairs, and a tall person with a full beard and man-bun, who wore a woman's pant suit and garish red lipstick with outrageous blue eyeshadow that would have done Tammy Faye Bakker proud. The atmosphere was chaotic and festive.

A slim, handsome Sikh man in an expensive suit and colorful turban made his way over and gripped Ray's hand. "Raymond! I'm so glad to see you!"

His soft voice carried the slightest hint of an accent.

"Mr. Singh, I want to introduce my friends. This is Nicholas, Clara and Michael."

"I am very pleased to meet you!" he exclaimed after shaking our hands. "I know that you are going to make me a very rich man!"

I gave Ray a confused look. "Mr. Singh is our CEO," he explained.

"And am I ever proud to have you fine young people on board!" He turned then, making his way to the side of the podium where he conferred with a stern, balding man in a grey suit. Mr. Singh pointed toward us and the man spoke into a lapel microphone. A moment later, another man in a similar suit approached and addressed Clara and me.

"Folks, if you could follow me a moment..."

We followed him down the sidewalk to a black Lincoln Navigator. He opened the back door and took a scarf off the rear bench seat.

"Ma'am, I'm going to ask your permission to place this hijab on you. Would that be OK? You can keep it afterward – it's only for the press photos."

"Well this is very exciting," Clara said, smiling at me.

He fitted Clara with the hijab, which looked quite fashionable and being of a sheer fabric, did little to cover her dazzling smile.

Then we followed him to the stage. He placed Clara to the right, and just behind the podium, and then stood me further away on the opposite side, between a small Chinese lady who might have been eighty-five years old, and a contorted woman with what I assumed was spina bifida, who sat sideways in a motorized wheelchair.

"When he says 'working together,' I want you to give a thumbs up. Make it look natural," the man said, before walking off the stage and back into the crowd.

From the corner of my eye, I noticed an LPC sign behind the stage with the slogan "Working together for women!" And then another government SUV pulled to the curb, and the prime minister climbed out of the back seat. The crowd broke into wild applause. Some of the news people applauded as well. With everyone holding up a cell phone, trying to get a video, it was a modern version of Beatlemania.

The prime minister's sleeves were rolled up to his elbows. A red tie hung loosely around his neck. He jogged up on the stage and shook hands with each of us in turn. He stopped at Clara, and seemed caught off guard. Instead of shaking his hand, she stood on her tiptoes, put a hand on each of his shoulders and kissed him on the cheek. "Good to see you, Clara," I heard him say. The news cameras snapped away furiously.

When he got to me, he grabbed my hand like we were old friends, and pulled me close. "Congratulations," he said. His breath smelled spicy like cinnamon and a bit like children's cough syrup. He didn't look sick. I wondered if it was some kind of expensive toothpaste only celebrities knew about.

Maybe "cough syrup" was the new "minty fresh."

"Congratulations for what?" I asked, but by then he had moved on to the lady in the wheelchair. He went to shake her hand, then seemed to realize she was quadriplegic. He mumbled something. It sounded like "what the fuck," but I couldn't be sure. He got down on one knee and pretended to speak to the woman who, for her part, smiled wondrously. He didn't appear to be actually saying anything, but his lips moved. I leaned closer, to hear, but no sound was forthcoming. I also couldn't help but notice the fine hairs on his cheeks had collected particles of a peach-colored dust. The prime minister was wearing pancake stage makeup. I only had a second to marvel at that before he finished with the handshaking and jogged to the podium.

"Mes amis, comment ça va?" he said. The crowd began applauding again. He waited a moment to let it die down.

"It's great to be here in beautiful Vancouver!" The applause took off again and he waited for it to fade. I couldn't see his face, but I could tell he was smiling winningly. I tried to smile too, and felt like I probably looked like an idiot. I'm not a natural smiler. I stopped smiling.

"This is a truly momentous occasion," the PM went on. "Today we are celebrating a real Canadian success story!

"When I heard that my close personal friend Ravi was dedicating his life to finding a hi-tech solution to women's health issues, I knew that this was a company I could get behind!

"A.I. Plus Womxn's Health Solutions not only promises to change the way we diagnose and treat breast cancer, it promises to change the way we go about the business of healthcare altogether. For too long, overpaid old men have tried to tell Canadian women how to live their lives, to get mammograms every other year, to go to the office for pap tests. And you know who profits from the business of healthcare?"

"Men!" someone in the crowd shouted.

The prime minister laughed. "You're beating me to my own punchlines!" Everyone erupted in hearty laughter.

"For too long, old conservative men have dictated the way we do business in Canada. Well, here's a newsflash. Canada belongs to the new generation now! Businesses like the one Ravi has started are going to drive us forward, into a better future. Look behind me, and you see men, women, and trans-gendered individuals from all walks of life coming together. Whether you're gay or straight, Jewish" – at this he gestured towards me – "or Muslim" – he gestured to one of the Syrian men down the line – "here at the threshold of a new Canada, we find ourselves working together!"

The crowd erupted again. To my left and right, I noticed everyone, including the woman I had assumed was quadri-plegic, giving a big thumbs up, and so I gave my own thumbs up and smiled my idiot smile.

The PM made a show of shaking everyone's hand one more time, then took Clara by the arm and they walked off the stage together. The man in the grey suit led her to one of the black SUV's and she climbed in the back. The PM took a moment with Mr. Singh, cutting a ceremonial ribbon in front of the main door, then got into the other vehicle and his entourage drove off down Cambie Street.

I found Ray. "I'm not Jewish," I said.

"I know," he said. "But you look Jewish."

"Why didn't they get an actual Jewish person?"

He looked at me the way a disappointed parent looks at a child who got a bad report card. "No grants," he said simply. I followed him and Michael into the foyer.

The lobby of the A.I. Plus Womxn's Health Solutions building was a vast atrium full of greenery and with a central water feature that burbled along under a footbridge. Natural sunlight filtered in from an enormous glass skylight four stories above us. The workspaces, it seemed, were relegated to the periphery of the atrium, circling it in glass enclosures, floor above floor. It reminded me of a grander interpretation of the Killiam Library at Dalhousie University.

A giant banner hung suspended over the atrium. "A.I. Plus Womxn's Health Solutions: This is a Green Space."

"Incredible," Michael said. "They've really gone all out!"

"What makes it a green space?" I asked Ray.

"Mostly that banner," he said.

"Really?"

"Look, it says right on it," he explained.

"It's an 'I think therefore I am' type of thing," Michael chipped in. "You'll get used to it."

Ravi Singh walked over to the water feature bridge. He was holding a wireless microphone. "How is everyone doing today?" he asked, his voice booming over speakers hidden amongst the plants.

Many people clapped, but I saw one group of Middle Eastern men and women – Syrians, I realized – drop to the floor, startled. They craned their necks, searching for the source of the loud noise.

Ray quick-stepped to the group, and whispered assurances, pointing out a few of the P.A. system's concealed speakers. One of the men smiled and nodded, but the women stood, brushing themselves off, and did not appear to be quite so amused.

"It's great to see so many beautiful faces in the crowd!" he said. "When we decided to start A.I. Plus Womxn's Health Solutions, we received a lot of applicants. I mean a lot!  And you folks are the cream of the crop! The very best of the very best!  Give yourselves a round of applause!"

A polite round of applause made its way around the room.

"When we began A.I. Plus Womxn's Health Solutions, we knew that we were about to boldly go where no business had gone before. By changing the paradigms of employment, and looking at our staff as investments instead of liabilities, we are opening the doors to a new tomorrow!"

After a short applause break, he continued. "Folks, I want

to introduce Mahmoud!  Mahmoud is an example of a made-in-Canada success story."

An olive-skinned man in jeans and an Adidas hoodie took the stage. He held up the microphone, but held it too close and a squeal of static briefly burst through the speakers.

"Hi everyone," the man's voice was painfully soft, and he was obviously deeply uncomfortable in the role of public speaker, "I'm Mahmoud,"

"Hi Mahmoud," someone in the crowd shouted.

Mahmoud armed beads of sweat from his forehead and produced a small sheet of paper from his pocket, then began reading. "Twelve months ago, my family and I were in a refugee camp in Istanbul. We had fled the fighting in Aleppo with only the clothes on our backs.

"When the Canadian government offered to bring me here, I jumped at the chance, even though it meant leaving my wife and four children behind in Turkey. Since coming to Canada, I have learned to write code in C++. When Mr. Singh offered me a job here, at first I thought there must be a mistake, since I hadn't yet finished my studies. But Mr. Singh believed in me, and hopefully soon, I will earn enough money to sponsor immigration for my wife and children. I am so grateful for this opportunity. Thank you."

A polite round of applause for Mahmoud settled when Ravi Singh took the microphone. "Isn't that great!" he exclaimed, clapping the side of the mic.

When he did this, a booming sound emanated from the speakers, and one of the Syrian women in front of me hit the deck again. This time, as she got to her feet, she let loose a long string of Arabic, which I interpreted to be swearing.

"Folks, your office assignments are explained on the screens around the atrium. Feel free to have a look around, and again, congratulations on your new jobs! If you are assigned to stations A through G, I have some good news and some bad news. The good news is, you have a couple of days off!

The bad news, unfortunately, is that we got a little bit behind in construction and your workspace isn't quite ready. Have no fear, your paychecks are still coming through. We'll send you a direct deposit every Wednesday, and will send out office updates via email to let you know when your space is available. For those in sections H and J, welcome to A.I. Plus Womxn's Health Solutions."

One last round of acclimation resounded through the giant atrium as Mr. Singh climbed down from the footbridge. Almost immediately, the Asian and Middle Eastern people began shuffling out the entrance and along the sidewalk outside. I found a screen and checked for my name. I was in section H, along with Ray, Michael and Clara. "Hey," I said to Ray, "we're all in section H together."

"Of course we are. That's how they do it. Teams live together in the apartments."

"You mean the company is putting all these people up in apartments?"

"It's the historical complex rejuvenation grant – the company owns the apartments, and gets government money for 'rejuvenating' them. If they're smart, they also get grants for putting workers with our income into the real estate boom that is Vancouver under the Corporate Middle Class Housing Subsidy for CREA Level 5 Real Estate Markets. By doubling the grant money, they can actually turn a pretty nice profit just by sitting on the properties. That's not to mention how much they get if they're housing any of the Syrians. That's some serious coin right there!"

"Incredible," I said.

"Isn't this great?" Michael said, gesturing toward the water feature.

I let my eyes wander around the glassed-out work enclosure. For a second I thought I was seeing an optical illusion.

"Guys – I see H – it's up there." I pointed to a sign over a cluster of cubicles. "But where are the stairs?  Or the elevator?"

"Wow," Ray said, looking genuinely impressed. "I'd heard about this, but I didn't think it could be done!"

"What am I looking at?" I asked.

"Follow the floor line," he said, pointing.

I followed his finger. Sure enough, the floor spiraled upwards such that one floor led naturally to the next without any stairs in between.

"It's the mother of all building code grants," Ray said. "The Code 19 Subsidy for Architecturally Progressive Accessibility. We must have funding for years!"

"Outstanding," said Michael, who led us to the inner door that opened into the cubicle spiral.

The slant in the floor was just discernable enough that it gave the impression you were leaning too far forward. As we spiraled up the workspace, past conference rooms and short-walled cubicle spaces, I felt ever-so-slightly seasick.

After five minutes, we arrived at zone H. Our pod of desks had been laid out with welcome baskets. I expected snack food, but when I opened one it was full of soap, toothpaste, shampoo, deodorant and a *Muscle and Fitness* magazine. I looked questioningly at Ray, but he just shrugged. Each chair had an all-in-one Macintosh computer in front of it. I had to hand it to Mr. Singh – it looked very modern.

I sat in a chair to test it out. It was comfortable and offered nice lumbar support, and when it faced the correct direction, the tilt of the floor was such that it felt very subtly like you were reclining in a lazy boy. The downside, however, was that if you rested your feet on the plastic base, the chair would roll downhill.

Ray noticed the same. "We're probably going to have to ask for some carpeting, or a rug," he said.

"Hey, where did Clara go?" Michael asked.

"She drove off in one of the PM's vehicles," Ray explained.

"No kidding."

"I think they're friends."

We opened our computers, thinking we might have an outlay of our tasks for the day, but they'd never been set up. We had to choose our own passwords, and I chose Dad112051, as I always did, because after losing him to cancer, I was perpetually worried I might forget his birthday.

As the computers had no Ethernet connection, we wandered around in search of a Wi-Fi router. I ran into Mahmoud in Zone J.

"Hi Mahmoud," I said, "I'm Nick."

"Hi Nick. It's a pleasure to meet you."

"Mahmoud, why isn't there a section I?  Why does it go from H to J?"

"I don't know," Mahmoud said.

"Mahmoud," Ray said, approaching. "Have you seen a wireless router?"

Mahmoud shook his head and turned and wandered off in the other direction.

"Mahmoud seems shy," I said.

"He'll come around, when Mahmoud strikes," said Ray.

"That was a pretty dry delivery," I said.

"I wasn't sure if it was racist. You can't be too careful these days," Ray said.

We never found the Wi-Fi router so we reconvened at Station H, and finished setting up our computers. I set a pen on the worktable and because of the tilt in the floor, it rolled off.

We found a washroom and helped ourselves to enough toilet paper to prop up the downward legs of the table and make a roughly even surface. Michael saw it as a good thing. "Depending on the kind of day you're having you can use your position at our worktable to make yourself feel bigger or smaller. Kind of like Alice in Wonderland, but on a more restrained scale."

Arranging the table took us through to ten o'clock. I noticed how quiet the office had become, and turned to Ray.

"Where is everyone?" I asked.

"Gone," he said.

"For the day?"

"Maybe," he said. "We'll see."

Ray browsed new business listings on Liftoff Capital on his phone, and Michael started scrolling through Tinder. I told him I'd never used Tinder before and he stared at me like I was from another planet. He decided to show me how it worked.

"It's pretty quiet right now," he said. He angled the screen so I could see – it showed a pretty Asian girl who had taken a selfie.

"She's cute," I said.

"You're not seeing it in context," he said.

He zoomed in the photo on the lower right corner of the screen. Clear as day, there was a toilet with a size XXL turd in it.

"Whoa," I said.

"It isn't the turd that's the problem," Michael explained, "it's what the turd says about her personality. See a lot of women on Tinder will only take a selfie after they have a shit – they think it makes them look skinnier. But when they're so keen to put themselves out there, even before they've managed to flush, it tells you they're desperate and they're going to be clingy. Who needs that?"

"So… this is a common occurrence?" I asked.

"Oh yes. I see one of these at least twice a day."

"Fascinating."


Mr. Singh approached, wearing a winning smile. "How are you, guys?  Did you get the computers working?"

"Yes, Mr. Singh. Thank you," Michael said.

"Terrific!  Did you figure out the Wi-Fi code?" he said.

"Not yet, Mr. Singh," Michael said.

"The code is Vancouver, with a capital V," he said.

"Thanks Mr. Singh," Michael said.

"Do you guys have any questions?"

"Yes, Mr. Singh," I said. "What are we doing?"

"This week, I want you and Ray to meet with a radiologist at the VGH. Team up with them for a research project and apply for a research grant."

"OK," I said. "What would you like us to research?"

"Well…" He scratched at his beard. "Whatever you can get a grant for, I guess. Something to do with women. And it should probably have something to do with technology. Tell the radiologist that we can fund the project. Tell them there will be a publication in it."

"So we're a research firm?" I asked.

"Sure," he said.

He looked searchingly toward the ceiling, and appeared to be in deep thought. "Maybe something with breast cancer," he said, then a moment later, "Or the uterus."

"What kind of budget are we going for?" I asked.

"Raymond will help you out," he said. "Do what Raymond recommends."

"OK" I said. "Mr. Singh – should it have something to do with artificial intelligence?"

"Most definitely."

"Because even by liberal estimates, there will be at least a few years before the first gen true neural network product cycle for complex medical applications has matured enough for market. And then, add to that, the questions of liability need solving."

"That's good," Mr. Singh said. "That should give us some time."

"Is there anything else you'd like us to do, Mr. Singh?" Ray asked.

"No, Raymond. Get the research grant application in as soon as you can."

"I understand," Ray said.

I took a moment, then turned again to Mr. Singh. "I'm not entirely clear on what our team does," I said. "Ray worked in software, and I have a medical background. Michael was in real estate. How do we all fit?" I asked.

"Listen – you guys are my A-team. You guys are going to make the eye candy that gets us noticed."

"What about all those other people who were here earlier? What do they do?" I asked.

"They are the B-team," he said.

"OK, but will we be working with them?"

"Oh no," Mr. Singh laughed. "That situation is too delicate. Plus, hardly any of them speak English yet."

"Mahmoud spoke English," I said.

"You guys are my A-team. My go-getters," Mr. Singh said, slapping my shoulder, apparently not having heard me.

He turned and began the long walk spiraling down the corridors of the A.I. Plus Womxn's Health Solutions building. Five minutes later, we watched him climb into a Bentley Continental and drive away.

Ray sat at his terminal. He motioned me to a seat beside him. "What's up?" I asked.

"I'm looking for our research partner," he said. He had the website open for the Department of Diagnostic Imaging at the Vancouver General Hospital.

"How do you know who to ask?"

"I'll know it when I see it," he said.

A moment later, he said "Bingo." He picked up the phone and dialed a number.

"Hi, I'm looking for Dr. Jennifer Chu. Yes, I'll hold."

Dr. Chu agreed to meet with us that afternoon, so Michael, Ray and I went for an early lunch of sushi. Michael ordered something called a Sunshine Philadelphia Roll, and he ate the spicy mayonnaise off the top, and the little cubes of cream cheese from inside. He drank two packets of soy sauce.

When we arrived at the VGH, Dr. Chu invited us into her

office. As it turned out, she had already designed a research project looking at the effect of computer-aided detection on the differentiation of lobular carcinoma vs ductal carcinoma in breast cancer patients. We signed mutual Non-Disclosure Agreements, which Ray had thought to bring, and I noticed that one of the blanks under "Parties" had been pre-populated with the name "Nova Health." I pointed this out to Ray. "Nice pickup," he said.

"Should we change it?"

"Why bother?"

We arrived back at the A.I. Plus Womxn's Health Solutions building at three o'clock, and we were the only people there. Magnetic plastic key cards were waiting for us at our workspace. They didn't have any names or information on them. They were just blank white cards.

Ray printed off a half-dozen grant applications, and handed three of them to me. "You fill these ones out, and I'll do these other ones."

My applications were as follows:

— British Columbia Women in Medicine Research Grant – The provincial government will offer up to $100,000.00 for any research project in medicine in which the research lead identifies as a female physician.

— British Columbia Visible Minorities in Medicine Research Grant – The Province of British Columbia is proud to offer a research grant with a value up to $75,000.00 for any medical research project in which the project lead identifies as a member of a visible minority group.

— The Canadian Visible Minorities in Medicine Research Grant – The Government of Canada is Proud to offer a federal research grant of up to $235,000.00 for any medical research performed, wherein the team lead identifies as a visible minority.

"Ray," I said, "all these projects say they need a budget. How much are you writing down?"

"Whatever the maximum number is for the grant."

"But it's totally different for each one," I said.

"I know. But under budget planning just change the number of 'expected study participants,' accordingly.

"Well, how much is it going to cost to actually do the study?"

"Come again?" he looked genuinely confused.

"What do you think the study will cost to do?"

"Nothing."

"What?"

"Weren't you listening to Dr. Chu? It's a retrospective analysis. She's having a resident do it already."

"So why are we involved in this at all?"

"Because it said on her department profile that she's a part-time researcher. That means she isn't a full-time clinical doctor. So, she has all these studies in her back pocket and she waits for 'research coordinators,' in this case, us, to come along and find her grant money. Once a grant has been coordinated, she gets paid for her research, and she publishes it. The research coordinator gets to add a project to the list of jobs they've completed, thereby justifying their job, and the grant people in government have managed to award their grants thereby justifying their own jobs. In this case, the research coordinators also make a fairly handsome profit for their company, and get to add a research project to their own list of corporate research. It's win-win-win-lose."

"Who loses?"

"The suckers who pay their taxes."

"So out of all these grants, how many do you think we'll get?" I asked.

"All of them," he said. "No question."

"But there's like three-hundred-ten thousand dollars in my pile."

"Yes," he said, "it's a pretty rich seam. I've got about two hundred more in this one."

"But we told Dr. Chu we could pay her up to fifteen thousand," I said.

Ray smiled.

"Why in the hell would she agree to that?"

"Two reasons," he said. "First, it's fifteen thousand dollars she otherwise wouldn't have made. Remember, this is a resident research project – a retrospective analysis no less. Real scientists don't put much weight behind them as they aren't all that valuable. Fortunately, the people in charge of handing out these grants are not scientists, nor are they concerned in any way about the value of the research being collected."

"OK."

"And two, she doesn't know about the existence of all these grants. Not only are they esoteric, but the government, either by default or design, is incapable of developing a functional website, therefore, only research coordinators like us are able to delve into their mess of an online presence and find these things."

The forms, essentially all the same, took an hour to fill out. Michael offered to do two – one from each of our piles – and it made for quick work.

We decided to walk home over the Cambie bridge. There were clumps of hair blowing from the railing. "What's with the hair?" I asked Michael.

"Environmentalists glued themselves to the bridge last week," he explained. "They wanted to disrupt traffic to end climate change."

"Oh."

We stopped at a post office to mail our research grant applications. When we emerged, a homeless man shuffled towards us. I thought he was going to ask for money, but to my surprise he called out, "Hey, Ray! Buddy! Wait up!"

"Oh shit," Ray said. "It's him!"

We waited while the man approached. He seemed pretty out of it.

"Ray," the man called out. "Ray Butler! You gonna help me, man?"

"I'm working on it!" Ray said.

"God bless you, Ray!" the man shouted. "God bless you, brother!" With that he turned and sprinted down the road. "Ray Butler, everyone!" he yelled. "That's THE Ray Butler!"

Once we'd turned the corner Michael said, "Is that the guy you told me about?"

"Yeah," Ray said.

"That's the homeless accountant," Michael said, looking at me. He was going to add more but Ray held up his hand to stop him. "Guys, let's not talk about him right now. I've got to do some thinking."

Michael and I did another grocery run. I began reading the labels on the condiments and tried to pick him something with nutritional value as a gift. I settled on Newman's Own Ranch Salad Dressing. When I rang it through for him, he seemed genuinely touched. Having read through the ingredients for so many condiments, I decided to invest in distilled vinegar should Michael's diet book ever reach publication.


We spent an hour on the roof, shooting pigeons and drinking wine (in Michael's case, cooking sherry). Ray was quiet and seemed lost in thought. He didn't even check his Liftoff Capital notifications.

After a while we decided to turn in. I wrote the day's passage up to and including the last sentence, when, at eleven o'clock, a topless pipeline protest erupted outside my apartment window. A group of three dozen or so half naked female protesters, covered in black paint made to look like oil, marched up Davie Street, hoisting a crucifix made of PVC pipe, upon which a fully naked female protester had been pseudo-crucified. A sign above the crucifee read "Mother Nature."

The protest was led by a federal politician. I'm not sure why, but all I could think about was whether protest groups qualified for federal and provincial grant money.

And thus, to the pounding of drums and megaphone chants, I retired for the evening.

## 3

*I THINK RAY HAS A SECRET LIFE.*

I woke up, needing to pee in the middle of the night, and I could hear him furiously typing away on his keyboard, swearing under his breath.

He either has a secret life or he was sleep-working.

# 4

Vegetable oil (soybean oil and/or canola oil)
Water
Buttermilk (milk)
Distilled vinegar
Sugar
Egg yolk
Garlic juice
Salt
Contains 2% or less of:
Buttermilk solids (milk)
Onion
Garlic
Natural flavor
Lactic acid
Xanthan gum
Lemon juice concentrate
Chives
Spice

*I AWOKE AND STRETCHED* and put on my exercise clothes. I left my room to find Ray in an agitated state, staring at seven or eight phone-book sized piles of documents scattered around our kitchen. He rubbed furiously at his temples.

"What's going on?" I asked.

"Hi Nick," he said. "Have you ever had the sudden certain feeling that your will is being subverted for nefarious purposes by some grand creator? Like your life has an author, and you are completely at their whim?"

"Sure," I said. "Why do you ask?"

"Are you running or walking this morning?"

"I dress up like I'm running, but I end up walking. It makes me feel exercised," I said.

"I'm coming with. Let's go."

We turned left at the bottom of Davie Street and walked past a series of bars along the waterfront. The route was a little disappointing compared to the morning before.

"I should explain about Lonnie," Ray said.

"OK."

"Lonnie was my accountant back in 2014 – really bright guy. He was a friend of mine, and so, I decided to take a chance and break my own golden rule of employment."

He stopped walking and stared out over the harbor, searching.

"Which was?" I prompted him.

"Never hire someone you have to pay. I make my living finding employment subsidy. I used to believe that there wasn't a single Canadian I couldn't find subsidy for. That was until I tried to find something for Lonnie.

"But I hired him anyway because we were friends, and because I needed an accountant. We tried a few things – I tried finding him a rural relocation grant because he was from Saskatchewan, but his area code was excluded. I tried to arrange a "Family members affected by domestic violence" subsidy, but try though we might, we couldn't find any persuasive evidence of a history of domestic violence going back generations. His great grandfather had resettled in Canada after the First World War, so I went for a "Family Members of Those Affected by Global Conflict" grant, but the entire First World War had been excluded. Can you imagine? It was terrifically unsettling."

"So what ended up happening?" I asked.

"What happened was I made two horrendous mistakes," Ray said. "Have you heard of those ancestry DNA tests you can get online?"

"Sure," I said.

"Well those were developed by the grand master of Grant and Subsidy Application. The way it works is, you spit in a little cup, and send it off to a DNA lab. The lab does a 'test,'" he said, using air quotes around the last word.

"The test comes back telling you which percentage of your DNA comes from which part of the world. That way, white European people like you can have your DNA tested and then prove to subsidy boards that we aren't just white European. For example, my test states I'm 12.5% sub-Saharan African."

"But you're saying the tests are bullshit."

"Even though we like to think the past is super-racist, you would have to be pretty dedicated to being a racist to turn down sex from a good-looking person of another race. Is it that hard to imagine that people from different races have been fucking away, often in secret, for time out of mind?"

I nodded.

"That's what makes identity politics so great!" Ray explained. "Basing grant applications on your racial identity means almost everyone can technically qualify, since our identities are almost all completely fluid. Let's face it – we're all the products of thirty-five thousand years of horny, usually drunk humans fucking one another."

"Except for Lonnie?" I asked.

Ray sighed. "That's right. Except for Lonnie. 100% White European. What are the odds?"

He sniffed. "I spent three years of my life on a coalition to lobby the government to accept the outcome of DNA testing in consideration of grant applications, and when they finally agreed to it, it ended up screwing over my best friend."

"But he was still your accountant, right? You just had to pay him?"

"Well, that's where my stupid pride came in," he said. "I found one incredible grant that had the possibility of making us both hundreds of thousands of dollars. It was called 'The Federal Subsidy for Recovering Opioid Addicts.' It would subsidize up to two hundred thousand dollars per year for hiring a certified professional – essentially a lawyer, accountant, dentist or engineer, who had suffered with and subsequently recovered from an opioid addiction."

"Oh Ray," I said, "you didn't."

"Yes, we did," he said. In a way, I think he was still proud of how ambitious he had been. I shivered.

"We got Lonnie hooked on smack. We used the safe injection site downtown, and every night for a week, we would go downtown and Lonnie would shoot up. It was supposed to stop after a week. That was the plan."

"What went wrong?" I asked.

"Two things. First – it turns out a heroin high is really incredible. Once Lonnie started, I couldn't convince him to do the rehab program. That's part of the subsidy, see. They have to go through rehab. And second, by the time Lonnie agreed to go to rehab, the fentanyl crisis was in full swing and there was a wait list two-years long. Not only that, but the federal regime changed, and the new government abandoned the subsidy!"

"Because it didn't affect enough people of color or something?" I asked.

"Oh God no, nothing like that. It isn't a racial thing. It was because they weren't giving out enough money. Turns out very few professionals who do a one-eighty and end up addicted to horse want to do a second one-eighty and go back to work as orthodontists. It's a pretty permanent type of decision."

"So what's the plan for Lonnie?" I asked.

"For now, he's happy to keep shooting up. He sleeps in the dog park under the Cambie Street Bridge. He says it's better than the place he had before he was homeless. I caught him offering blowjobs for oxycontin a few months ago. I offered to put him up in an apartment and to privately pay for a rehab place anywhere in the world, to get him back up and running as a contributing member of society, but he said he'd rather give oral sex for drugs than fill out T4 forms for grocery money."

"I don't care much for filing my taxes either," I said.

"Ever since things fell apart, I've been lobbying to get the subsidy replaced. I think if there were the promise of free government money in it, it might give Lonnie a sense of purpose, and help him find the road to recovery."

"Why don't you ask Clara?" I said. "She seems to be on friendly terms with the prime minister."

Ray stopped walking for a second. "That's not a bad idea," he said. "Thanks Nicholas."


Nothing happened at work today. Well, nearly nothing happened. We found a kitchen at the very top of the building. Ray explained that it was likely part of the "Healthy Workforce Initiative," a handsome government subsidy for employers who encourage their employees to exercise.

"By putting the kitchen at the top of the spiral, they've probably paid for the lease on the building," he explained.

Michael was disappointed that there were no condiments in the refrigerator, so he and I went to Costco and bought two hundred dollars of salad dressing, relish, mustard and hot sauce.


At four o'clock my mother called.

"Your brother wants to go visit you in Vancouver," she said.

"How's his foot?" I asked.

"The doctor says he needs to wear a special boot for three weeks."

"Well, he can come out if he wants, but we kind of have to walk everywhere. I don't have a car."

I heard her cover the receiver with her hand and yell, "Jeffrey! He says he doesn't have a car. You would have to walk. Why don't you stay here with me?"

I heard a muffled response.

"I should have known better. He says he wants to see you."

"Well, I'm here," I said. "He can come any time."

"Great," she said. "Nobody ever wants to visit mom. I feel like chopped liver." She hung up.

When we got home, Clara was sleeping on the couch. She was lying under a fuzzy blanket, and looked like a child who had dozed off in the middle of a dinner party.

We didn't want to wake her so we walked to a Thai restaurant. We ordered pad thai, and Michael had to suck the peanut sauce off the noodles. He left a side plate of bone-white noodles beside his main plate. It was exciting to watch.

"That was exquisite," he said after we paid the bill.

"How come you don't poop?" Ray asked.

"I don't know," Michael said. "Maybe it's the condiments. Sometimes I feel like there's some external force that's weirdly authoring my existence, and that force has just decided that I don't need to poop."

Ray and I exchanged a startled look. Michael didn't seem to notice.

"I don't mind," he said. "Pooping is incredibly time consuming. The toilet is also where I did all my online shopping. It got so expensive! I'm happy with the new me."

"You always seem happy, Michael," I said.

"Interesting," he said. "I don't think of myself as a particularly happy guy. You know what I bet it is?"

"Ritalin?" Ray asked.

Michael looked surprised. "Yes!" he said. "Ritalin! How did you know I started taking Ritalin?"

"I saw your pill bottle."

"Well, that's impressive detective work," Michael said. "About two years ago, I was going through a rough patch. I hadn't had a sale in a while, and so I was without commission. I play up my freegan days like they were inspired by nutritional curiosity, but truth be told, I was house poor! I'd picked up this gorgeous Kitsilano two-storey for two-point-seven mil, and then my sales dried up. It was really a scary time.

"I didn't know where to turn, but my friend Wu Chung

suggested I try Ritalin. He said it would help me focus. And let me tell you guys, it was like the scales fell from my eyes. I had been looking at the world through a glass, but darkly as they say. Suddenly, everything became unbelievably clear. My sales picked up, I bought my house outright – the world was my oyster once again. Only…"

"You were lonely," Ray said.

"That's right. I was terribly lonely. It was the one puzzle in my life that Ritalin couldn't solve. But it did give me the idea of applying to companies with group housing. And I met you guys. So I guess I have Ritalin to thank for solving it after all."

"Wait," I said. "Are you saying the Ritalin is actually making decisions for you? Uh, I'm not sure that's healthy, Michael."

"It sure feels that way," he said.

"Right now, am I talking to Michael, or Michael's Ritalin?" I asked.

"Gosh," he shrugged, "it's kind of hard to tell."

"What an unusual conversation this is," I said. "There's a distinct possibility that I'm talking to a chemical."

"We're always talking to chemicals," Ray said.

"That's a good point," Michael said.

When we got back to the apartment, Clara was gone. We went to the roof to drink cooking sherry, and kill rock pigeons.


Things I learned about air-rifles tonight:

    — In Canada, air rifles can fall into the restricted or non-restricted category.

    — Non restricted air rifles are not allowed to fire a pellet faster than 500 feet per second.

    — Restricted and non-restricted air rifles are usually the same rifle with a different sized spring inside.

    — The springs can be purchased on eBay for less than one dollar.

    — Converting a non-restricted air rifle to a restricted

air rifle requires a Phillips head screwdriver and approximately thirty-two seconds of manual labor.

— A restricted air rifle is significantly more humane for dispatching rock-pigeons.

— There have been no reports in the history of Canadian online air rifle forums of an officer of the law producing a ballistic chronograph to test whether a non-restricted air rifle is firing at or below the speed specified by the manufacturer.

— The restriction of air rifles is universally considered to be an irritating nuance of life as a citizen of Canada.

# 5

Distilled vinegar
Water
#1 Grade mustard seed
Salt
Turmeric
Paprika
Spice
Natural flavors
Garlic powder

*I CAUGHT A BRIEF GLIMPSE* of Mahmoud today. He was carrying a Costco-sized container of Charmin two-ply toilet paper into the men's room. When he saw me, he panicked and left the building. He shouldn't have. I was weary of A.I. Plus Womxn's Health Solutions' use of environmentally friendly toilet paper. It might generate some grant money, but it felt like it could give you splinters.

In the total vacuum of instruction, Michael decided to rewrite *Green Eggs and Ham* with a socially conscientious twist, in order to reach out to disenfranchised youth and excite within them the desire to read.

Ray, having nothing better to do, submitted Michael's work for consideration of the "Canadian Street Poet Bursary." He also phoned his own celebrity friend, Douglas Coupland, who was busy working on an art project called "The two-thousand-dollar blanket," in which he was sewing one-thousand Canadian two-dollar coins to a blanket.

"I don't get it," I admitted to Ray. "What qualifies Douglas Coupland as a national treasure?"

"Three hyphenated words," Ray explained with pauses between each word. "Public-Private-Partnership."

Clara came to work around lunchtime. She entered the building with Mr. Singh. I caught up with them in the atrium.

"Hi guys," I said.

"Oh hi, Michael," Mr. Singh said.

"I'm Nicholas," I said.

"Sorry Nicholas. There are so many new faces. Sometimes it's tough to keep them straight."

I looked around. There was nobody else in the building. Then I saw three stories up, Michael was standing in the window. He smiled and waved. I'm considering calling him Michael's Ritalin from now on. I waved back.

"That's OK, Mr. Singh," I said. "I was just wondering if there's anything you'd like me to do. We finished the research grant applications yesterday – we're working on a study that looks at the usefulness of computer aided diagnosis in differentiating lobular carcinoma from invasive ductal carcinoma."

"That's great, Michael," he said.

"I'm Nicholas, Mr. Singh," I said.

"Oh right. Sorry." He stared around the atrium for a minute then closed his eyes like he was concentrating. I wondered if he was going to ask which CAD algorithm we were using in the study. I was concerned because we'd forgotten to ask Dr. Chu.

"What are those big goldfish called?" he said. "You know, the ones you see in ponds at rich peoples' houses?"

"Koi?" I asked.

"Yeah – those are the ones. Can you guys pick up, let's say, three hundred koi for our water feature?"

"Um, sure," I said. "You know I'm a medical doctor, right? I can do research for you and whatnot."

"Just the koi for now, Michael."

"Yes sir, Mr. Singh. We'll get right on it."

"Do you want company?" Clara asked.

"Sure," I said.

"Can we have some money to rent a van, Mr. Singh?" she asked, her voice sugary sweet.

"Anything for my A-team," he said and handed her a TD Platinum Infinite corporate credit card.

"What do you know about koi?" Clara asked after we'd left the building.

"They look like big goldfish," I offered.

"Right. But where do you go to buy them?"

"I'll have to Google it," I said. But Google was not forthcoming with an immediate answer. I called a few pet stores but they weren't helpful.

"Let's get the van, then have cocktails and think this through," Clara suggested.

"OK," I said.

We took the sky train to the airport and talked along the way. Clara made lovely, polite conversation, but I got the distinct impression I wasn't so much speaking to her as I was speaking to her representative alter ego. After all the raw honesty I'd experienced with Ray and Michael's Ritalin, I have to admit, it was quite refreshing.

"So are you really a doctor," she asked, "or is it, like, one of Ray's loophole things?"

"No, I'm a doctor," I said.

"So what's up with that? Why is Dr. Nick out here buying koi for the A.I. Plus Womxn's Health Solutions water feature?"

"It's kind of a long story," I said.

She looked suddenly concerned. "Oh God, you didn't feel someone up during a Pap test, did you?"

"No, no, nothing like that."

"Did you hesitate before you said 'no?' I couldn't tell."

"I don't think so," I said.

"So what happened?"

"It's hard to explain."

"Try to explain it with one word," she said.

"Cancer," I said.

"Oh shit. You got cancer?"

"No," I said, "not me. Not that I know of."

"Who?"

"Everyone else. I mean literally everyone. All of my patients. At first, I thought it was just a coincidence. I was getting lab and X-ray reports back. Two in a row. Then three. Then five. Then thirty. I started freaking out. Men – women – children – all of them. Every test started coming back positive for cancer. Lymphoma, Leukemia, breast, lung, colon, pancreas, brain. It went on like that for three days. Then my dad was diagnosed with stage four pancreatic cancer. It was like a nightmare I couldn't wake up from. It went on like that for months. Dad passed, and I became afraid to order tests on anyone, knowing what the results were going to be. Psychiatrists would call that 'magical thinking,' only, it wasn't really. Because I'm pretty sure that if I ordered blood work on someone, even today, like any random person off the street, it would diagnose them with leukemia.

"Finally, I just took it as a sign from God, and quit. After four years of college, four years of med school and five years of residency and a one-year fellowship, I quit after six months."

"Wait a minute," Clara said, "that's totally crazy."

"Right?"

"Are you saying you believe in God? That's so, nineteen forties!"

"Oh," I said, "I thought you meant the cancer thing."

"No," she said. "The God thing."

We didn't speak again until we reached the Enterprise counter.

We rented a van. The man at Enterprise asked if we were a couple, and Clara said, "Of course we are," and draped her arm around my shoulders. She was probably only ten years younger than me, but I felt, at that moment, old enough to be her father.

As we drove back to Vancouver, I asked her why she said

we were a couple.

"Well, he was screening you."

"Screening me? As in, security screening?"

"Uh huh. He wanted to make sure you weren't a radical incel. It's part of their job description."

"Incel?"

"An involuntary celibate – like that lunatic who drove a Ryder van over all those people in Toronto. Basically they're men that can't get laid. And apparently some of them have organized into a terrorist movement."

"Huh," I said. "It seems like there's a movement for everything nowadays."

"You can say that again," she said.


We went to a place called Uva for cocktails. It had been a while since I'd ordered a cocktail, so I ordered a whisky sour. But when it came, I was surprised, because I had it confused with a Tom Collins. I think it was the "sour" part of the name that threw me off. I acted like it was no big deal though. Clara had a Cosmopolitan.

"Hey, that reminds me of *Sex and the City*," I said, when her drink arrived.

"Do I remind you of Sarah Jessica Parker?" she asked.

"Not particularly, no."

"Good," she said, "Because I think Sarah Jessica Parker kind of looks like a horse."

"She's kind of pretty," I said. Secretly though, I thought she did look like a horse. But I didn't want to get into criticizing people for the way they looked. I look like a homeless Jewish potato.

"Pretty in a 'My Pretty Pony' way I guess," Clara said.

"Say, this isn't bad. Want to try it?" I asked, offering my drink.

"Did you mean to order a whisky sour?" she asked, eyeing me suspiciously.

"Tom Collins," I admitted. "Am I that obvious?"

"Here," she said, "switch with me."

To my relief, her cosmopolitan was much more to my taste.

"You're not very self-conscious, are you, Nick?"

"It goes away as you get older," I explained.

"I don't know," she said. "I've spent time with a lot of self-conscious men, and a lot of them are older than you."

"Yeah, but you hang out with celebrities," I said. "They have to care what people think of them. It's how they make their living. Speaking of which, what's the deal with you and the prime minister?"

"Oh," she said, "we're friends. I went surfing with him in Tofino yesterday."

"That's pretty neat," I said, not knowing what else to say.

"Now he is a self-conscious guy," she said. She slugged back the rest of the whisky sour, and motioned to the waitress for another. The waitress looked confused because that wasn't the drink Clara had started with. "We switched!" she shouted.

The waitress nodded like she got it, and went to the bar.

"He doesn't seem self-conscious on TV," I said.

"You know what he did last night?"

"What?"

"Shit – actually, I can't tell you. And that's not because I don't like you. I think you're OK, even with all that God bullshit. But I had to sign an NDA."

"Your friend, the prime minister, made you sign an NDA to hang out with him?"

"No," she said, "his handlers do it. It's standard protocol."

"What about Hulk Hogan and Peter Mansbridge?" I asked.

"Oh, they're pretty laid back. They don't do the NDA thing, even though it bit Hulk Hogan in the ass a few years ago. He's pretty easy going."

"What's his real name," I asked.

"It's Terry, but he likes it when you call him 'Hulk.' A lot of these guys are like that. Even though I've known the prime minister for years, he likes to be called Mr. Prime Minister. It's like they live within their alter egos."

Her second drink came.

"What does Peter Mansbridge like to be called?"

"Peter Mansbridge," she said, "but like that, with the whole first and last name."

"Interesting," I said. "Why do you know all these celebrities?"

"I met them through my old line of work."

"Were you in media?" I asked.

"Why did you guess that?"

"You look camera-friendly," I said.

"Oh, that's a nice thing to say," she said. "My background is actually more media relations."

"Did you know Mr. Singh before all this?" I asked.

"I'd met him a few times over the last year – our work directed us to the same social circles. He's incredibly good at finding money, as you've probably figured out by now."

"Yes, he seems to leave no stone unturned. It's an unusual business, isn't it?"

"What is?"

"Well, A.I. Plus Womxn's Health Solutions."

"Is it?" she asked. "I haven't even been in yet."

"I'll give you an example," I said. "We have this huge, modern building, but I've never seen anyone but our own team working there. On the first day, Mr. Singh said some of the offices weren't ready, but still, I would have thought some of the other workers would come in. Or people doing construction on those offices. But no – it's just H-section and Mahmoud – he's in J-section. There's no I section. And while we applied for a study grant, that did in fact have something to do with women's' health, we haven't done anything since. OK, actually, Michael showed me how Tinder works. But other than that, we haven't done anything useful. Today, for example, our job is to find koi. I have thirteen years of post-secondary education and I'm shopping for decorative fish."

She paused to see if there was more. "Well, that all sounds pretty normal to me," she said, "but I'm used to Vancouver."

She gave the waitress Mr. Singh's credit card for the cocktails and used her phone to call the Canada Koi Club of British Columbia, which is a real club, and which meets the third Sunday (except holidays) of every month in the greater Vancouver area. The president of the Canada Koi Club of BC answered on the first ring. He directed us to a company called West Point Trading Company, which he assured us could meet our every koi-related need.

Next, she called West Point Trading Company, and when a man answered the phone, she looked amused and checked her screen to confirm something.

"What?" I asked.

"Same guy," she whispered.

Clara got directions, and we made the drive in half an hour. I was nervous driving the big van in traffic. The east side seemed a little more chaotic. Eventually we came to a residential street. The West Point Trading Company was a small Vancouver style split-level home. There was no indication or sign to suggest it was a business, or in particular, a koi fish farm.

A man answered the door and introduced himself as George Nakamato. "Ah, come in guys," he said in a cultured diplomatic James Bond villain voice, "you're here for the koi, right?"

"Yes, Mr. Nakamoto," Clara said, "we spoke on the phone."

"Great, great," he said. "Leave your shoes here, and follow me downstairs."

We did. As we descended the stairs to the basement, I detected a faint musty smell. "So how many koi are you looking for?" he asked.

"Three hundred," Clara said.

"Oh," he said. "That's a lot."

"Is that a problem?" I asked.

"Well, I have three," he said. "But I can get more! Give me two months, and I can get three hundred. Do you want show-quality koi? I can get show quality – imported from Tokyo. They're the best of the best!"

"Well, let's have a look at the ones you have," Clara said.

George led us to an aquarium at the back of the basement. Three white and orange piebald fish swam in lazy circles.

"How much for these three?" She asked.

"Well, these are Kohaku – show quality. Nine inches each. I can give them to you for fifteen dollars an inch."

"Do you take credit cards?" she asked.

I felt a little ridiculous driving back to A.I. Plus Womxn's Health Solutions in the big rented moving van with a single small bucket of three koi fish between Clara's feet. I mentioned it to her, and she offered to put them in the back of the van if it would make me feel better.

"No," I said. "It's OK."

"I have an idea," she said. She directed me to a Home Depot on Cambie Street. "I'll be right back," she said and ran in.

She came back out with a stack of a dozen buckets, then explained her idea.

"It seems a little zany," I said.

"Now there's a word you don't often hear in day-to-day conversation," she said. "Zany."

"That's makes two. The other day it was 'horrendous,'" I explained.

"I'm going to make an effort to use more unusual words," she declared. "It will be uproarious."


We went to the Heathman Lodge Hotel first. There was an extravagant koi pond in the foyer. Clara led the way to the front desk and asked for the manager.

She explained to the manager, whose name tag said "Tina"

that we were with the department of fisheries and oceans, and that we were investigating a Koi Flu outbreak in Vancouver and trying to trace it back to its source. If we could temporarily borrow five or six of their fish for further study, it would be greatly appreciated.

Tina helped us scoop them into a bucket.

We repeated this process at the Telus Garden Building, the Fairmont Pacific Rim, the Dr. Sun Yet Sen Chinese Botanical Garden, and several Richmond Car dealerships. In all, we stole sixty-one koi, and purchased three.

By the time we arrived at A.I. Plus Womxn's Health Solutions, it was full dark. I used my key card to open the door, and we took turns carrying buckets of koi to the water feature. After dumping my sixth or seventh bucket, I stopped and asked Clara, "Do they need specific water conditions?"

She Googled it. "We're probably fine for now," she said.

When we finished dumping the fish, we stacked the buckets (i.e., the evidence of our crime spree) under the dead space that subtended the rising office space floor. I'd left my laptop upstairs so I jogged up the spiral to retrieve it. Then I jogged back down. Say what you will, I was getting exercise.

We returned the van and took the Canada line back to our apartment.

Michael's Ritalin met us at the door. "Oh hi guys," he said. "Great news, I was able to have a bowel movement."

He jogged off for the elevator.

"Lucky bastard," Clara said.


My brother Jeff arrived about an hour ago. He's wearing a walking boot. It clunks loudly everywhere he goes. He told me he needs to sleep on the bed because of his foot injury so it looks like I'm on the couch.

I haven't watched television since I got here. I don't know what's happening with the world. Frankly there isn't much I can do about it. I'm not sure why I cared so much before.

I can't sleep, so here is a non-comprehensive list of words that you rarely hear in conversation but occasionally see in print:
— Adjudicate
— Apprehensive
— Barmaid
— Clairvoyant
— Curmudgeonly
— Dastardly
— Delightful
— Dexterous
— Droll
— Fastidious
— Ghastly
— Horrendous
— Imbecilic
— Juxtaposition
— Lackadaisical
— Lamentable
— Magnificent
— Nefarious
— Opulent
— Pantomime
— Querulous
— Rapacious
— Steadfast
— Tribulations
— Uproarious
— Vacuous
— Vetted
— Waspish
— Whimsical
— Zany

6

*Jeff went shopping today with Michael's Ritalin. Because my brother is portly and ashamed and because Michael's Ritalin needs real-life success stories in order to make the book a best seller, the two hit it off right away. Michael's Ritalin's perky, upbeat personality also help offset Jeff's depression after doing chores around the house for Mom, and suffering his foot injury.*

*WHEN I ARRIVED AT* A.I. Plus Womxn's Health Solutions, there was a grant application form on our workstation from the Department of Fisheries and Oceans – the maximum grant allowable was 2.7 million dollars earmarked for studying the indoor farming of non-native fish species in inland environments.

I wrote up a research proposal related to our koi pond, and decided to add "The additional study of the efficacy of farming invasive species such as Asian carp in inland farming environment, and its safety and risk-profile in relation to the Pacific salmon fishery." I ran it by Ray, feeling quite proud of myself, but he managed to nearly double the total ask-value by using names selected from our list of employees that had first-nations people's undertones, and by specifically describing our office building as being within the boundaries of unceded territory. He's a bloodhound who smells out government money. I made a note in the calendar on my phone to go fishing for non-koi Asian carp.

The koi pond was a smash hit! Our workgroup, minus Michael's Ritalin, ate lunch in the atrium, watching the fish.

At one o'clock, Michael's Ritalin and Jeff made their way up to H-section. Jeff was excited. "Do you know about the umbrellas?" he asked me.

I saw that it was raining. "The dumpster thing?"

"Yeah! Well Michael and I came up with an idea to turn that into an app – we'll put bins all over the city and when you leave your umbrella in one, you mark it on the app so it keeps track of the total umbrella inventory. When you pick one up, you mark it down too, you see?"

"I bet we can get an Environment Canada grant," said Michael's Ritalin.

"Holy Saint fucking Francis!" exclaimed Ray.

He spun his chair to face his workstation, and began typing frantically.

"What are you doing?" I asked.

"Building the app!" he said. He wouldn't say anything else for the whole afternoon. It was the most focused I'd seen him, including the time we met Lonnie. Truth be told, I was surprised he could actually program software like that. I'd suspected his programming skills were at the "for-grant-application-purposes-only" level.

Jeff, Clara, Michael's Ritalin and I sat by the koi pond while I finished the Fisheries and Oceans application for our koi-pond-cum-experimental-fish-farm. Ray came bounding down the spiral at four o'clock. "You're all programmers," he said. He uploaded the app Umbreller to our phones. "You guys have the master copies," he said, "so you have to mark anywhere you put an Umbrella can. Now let's get moving!"

They waited five minutes by the koi pond while I ran up the spiral to retrieve my briefcase.

We mailed my grant application, along with three applications for Umbreller – one to the Ministry of Environment and Climate Change, one to Technology British Columbia, and one to Environment Canada.

"Where to next?" I asked.

"I need to find Lonnie," Ray said. "You guys need to find receptacles for umbrellas and start placing them around town!"

Clara and I returned to the office and retrieved our koi buckets from the dead space under the spiral, and Michael's

Ritalin and Jeff agreed to place them around town and mark their locations on Umbreller.


Wu Chung called Michael's Ritalin while we were having dinner. We had Italian, at my request, as I hoped the vitamin C in the tomato sauce would offset the latent scurvy in Michael's Ritalin's body. I was also concerned for Jeff, who, over the course of twenty-four hours, had decided to fully embrace the condimenting lifestyle.

Wu Chung invited Michael's Ritalin to a party on his boat. There seemed to be a lot of boat parties happening.

"You guys can come too," Michael's Ritalin said. "Wu said he'd love to meet you!"

"Can we fish off the boat?" I asked.

Until we arrived, the party on Wu Chung's mega yacht had been attended only by formally dressed Chinese nationals, and it had the appearance of the opening scene from Indiana Jones and the Temple of Doom.

I arrived wearing cargo shorts, and carrying a fishing rod and tackle box. Wu Chung met us at the gang plank.

"What's the deal, here," he said, eyeing Jeff and I. Then his gaze found Clara. "Oh, hi Clara."

"Hi Wu."

"I was hoping to use this party as a dual-purpose event, both to network and to fish for Asian carp for our koi pond," I explained.

"Ah – the Department of Oceans and Fisheries grant?" he asked.

"The very one," I said.

He smiled. "Welcome aboard, friends!"

While the party got into swing, I dangled my legs off the swim deck and jigged a twister tail chartreuse rig along in the mega-yacht's wake. I snagged two fish under the Lion's Gate bridge, and a third at the mouth of the harbor. I wasn't 100%

sure they were Asian carp, but they were a close enough match to the photos I found on Google Images, that I decided they would do.

I realized we might have a salinity problem between the carp and the koi, but since koi are a form of Asian carp themselves, I guessed we'd probably be alright.

Wu Chung, in his tuxedo, sat down next to me. He smoked a long, thin cigar, and between puffs, he examined my bucket of silver fish.

"What is it you do, Nicholas?" he asked.

"I'm a medical doctor. What line of work are you in, Mr. Chung?"

"Import/export," he said. "Did you happen to steal some koi from the Shangrila Hotel yesterday afternoon?"

"Yes sir," I said. "How did you know?"

"Those were my koi; I own that hotel."

"I'm sorry, Mr. Chung," I said. "I'm sure I can get them back for you."

"No, no," he said, clapping me on the back. "I like your initiative. I'm one of Ravi's investors. Did Michael tell you?"

"He didn't mention it, no."

"Ravi has a nose for government money. It's a true gift. So if he needs koi, I say let him have my koi. Koi may bring us peace, but money brings us koi, among other things, so it is my opinion that we should pursue the money first."

"That's a good way of looking at it," I said.

"Nicholas," he sighed, "if you could have anything in the world what would you have?"

"Wisdom," I said.

"Good answer. Do you know what I would have?"

"Power?" I asked.

"Happiness," he said. "I know a lot of wise men. But none of them seem to be happy. In fact, many of them are downright miserable."

"Maybe they aren't wise enough," I said.

"I don't know," Wu said. "Anyway, nice meeting you."

I kept fishing until the party ended. It was nice to have a linear task in a non-linear time. Aside from a brief catfight between two supermodels in ball-gowns, and my brother Jeff drunkenly tossing his walking boot into Vancouver Harbor, things stayed more or less on track for a few blissful hours.

When we got back to the apartment, black Lincoln Navigators were curbed up beside the main entrance.

"Oh shit," Clara said.

*I'm going to take a break here. That was a lot to write. It's now 5:30 in the morning, and I need to get an hour's sleep. We'll call it "building literary tension," instead of authorial laziness. But I am lazy. And since I'm likely the only person who will ever read this journal, I hereby express my contempt for any future readers who consider this tension-building device to be shallow or transparent.*

# 7

Water
Canola oil
Vinegar
Modified corn starch
Whole eggs and egg yolks
Sugar
Salt
Lemon juice
Xanthan gum
(Sorbic acid, calcium disodium EDTA used to protect quality)
DL alpha tocopheryl acetate (vitamin e)
Phosphoric acid
Natural flavors
Citric acid
Oleoresin paprika
Beta-carotene (for color)

*HAVE YOU EVER LOOKED* at your life from the outside and wondered how one-dimensional you must seem to the people around you? I don't think there's anything wrong with being a one-dimensional being, other than the obvious issue of objectification, but personally, I don't mind being objectified if it makes it easier for people to relate to me. I used to portray "hard worker" as my dominant characteristic. I figured if other people saw me as a uni-dimensional object, the single character trait I would want them to associate with me was that I was the guy who worked hard.

But times they are a-changing. Hard work is no longer the path to success or reverence. Aren't those the things we all secretly crave? Money and the chance to be revered? But in this new world, those things seem to come to the people who pretend not to want them. In fact, they seem to actively fall upon those who work the least, but who happen to have appealing facial symmetry. I'm not complaining. I'm just stating the facts as they lie.

Also, I'm feeling a little guilty about calling Michael "Michael's Ritalin," because it objectifies Michael. But when I mentioned it to him he said he thought it was "Great. Kind of quirky!" And stated that he "liked it." He also said, "For the record, Nicholas, I'm pretty sure I really am Michael's Ritalin. Michael and I are pretty different."

I'm worried I'm creating a personality schism.

But where Michael's Ritalin seems to be "the upbeat, quirky guy," and Ray is the "wizened business-savvy guy," and Clara is the "mysterious fun lady," and Jeff is "the Frumpy, fun-loving brother character," where does that leave me? "Hard-working-guy" is in the garbage bin forever. It wasn't fun and there was no pay-off. So what quality should I make the dominant one? The old guy? The poor guy? That's probably where I stand right now. How do I become the "fun to be around" guy? Or the "always helpful" guy? Do I even want to be that person?

If I'm sounding philosophical it's because I spent the night trying to talk the prime minister down from a children's cough syrup induced existential crisis.

What happened is this:

When we came back from Wu Chung's yacht party, a group of men in grey suits were waiting for us – or more specifically, for Clara. Their role, though it was never fully clarified, is basically the Canadian equivalent of the secret service. They protect the prime minister, but despite their better judgment, they also have to serve the prime minister. They are obliged to obey him. And last night, apparently, he got smashed on his favorite cocktail, The Flaming Homer, which he styled after Homer's famous cocktail from the episode of the Simpsons that goes by that name. The prime minister's version contains grape-flavored children's cough syrup with a high dose of dextromethorphan. Some parents don't care so much about the cough, it seems, as they do about knocking their children unconscious. I'm all in on that one. What kid couldn't use a good night's sleep, interrupted though it may be by DM-induced psychosocial nightmare content?

The PM, it was later explained to me, began making Flaming Homers as a joke during a room crawl in his college days, but has since developed a genuine cough syrup addiction.

At any rate, he insisted that his security detail locate Clara, and deliver him to her. So along with the cough syrup thing, we learned that the PM is head-over-heels infatuated with our roommate.

He was sitting on our couch, dipping into a jar of pickled eggs (with his bare hands), and crying when the security agents allowed us into our own apartment.

The man who had put me on the stage for the grand opening of A.I. Plus Womxn's Health Solutions was there. He asked each of us to sign an NDA, but he knew it was a lost cause. The PM was making a real scene.

"Clara," he said, when he saw us, "I love you!  I can't stop thinking about you. Please come away with me."

The grey-suited security men, looking embarrassed, stepped outside, into the hallway. The man I'd recognized was the last one out. He made a hand motion to me, that I interpreted as "I'll be standing right here, so just yell if you hear small arms fire kicking off." Then he gently closed the door.

Clara, for her part, played it cool. "Mr. Prime Minister," she said, "you're having a cough syrup induced existential crisis again."

"Babe," he said, "*je t'aime!*"

"Let's talk about it in the morning, Mr. Prime Minister. I'm really tired." She then went to her room, leaving just us guys in the common area.

The apartment was filled with an awkward silence, until Michael's Ritalin offered the prime minister a glass of cooking sherry. He accepted it, and drank it greedily.

"There you go," Michael's Ritalin said, "that should help take the edge off."

"Thanks," the prime minister said.

"Are those pickled eggs?" Jeff asked.

"Now Jeff," Michael's Ritalin warned, "you don't want to break the diet on the first day."

"Right, right," Jeff said. "Is that brine or vinegar?"

"Vinegar," sniffed the prime minister.

"Mind if I help myself to a glass?"

"Sure." He handed Jeff the jar of pickled eggs. Jeff poured some of the supernatant off into a coffee cup and tried a sip. He poured a measure of cooking sherry into the mix and tried again. "Hey, that's pretty good!"

He made it halfway to the washroom before he crumpled to the ground and began snoring. In Jeff's defense, he was still on East Coast time. Michael's Ritalin got up and helped him into my bed. That seemed slightly unfair since Jeff had thrown his walking boot into Vancouver Harbor, but I figured he would be more crippled from his inevitable hangover than he would be from the probably-mostly-healed foot hole. I didn't want to guess how much cooking wine and sherry he'd had on Wu's boat. I supposed he could keep the bed another night.

I was tired, but the prime minister was sitting on the couch, which was my *de facto* bed. "So," I said, trying to make polite conversation. "What's it like being Prime Minister?"

"It's OK," he said. He seemed to have gone from weepy to blank. I think the cooking sherry was introducing itself to the cough syrup.

"Just OK? It seems to me like you enjoy it. All the women's stuff, and whatnot. Seems like you're getting your agenda out there."

"Oh," he said, "haha."

"What?"

"Did Clara tell you?"

"She told me you were friends, you went surfing together."

"But not about the project?"

"No, Mr. Prime Minister. She didn't mention any project."

"That's good. She's a nice girl. Did she say anything else about me? Do you think she likes me?"

"I don't know," I said. "She didn't have anything negative to say."

"Super," he said. He put his hands behind his neck and leaned back to watch the TV. The television was turned off. He might have been watching the reflection of our ceiling fan on the blank screen. It was hard to tell from where I was sitting. He seemed to be enjoying it.

My position was awkward. I had spent years really disliking the man. But I had assumed he was politically passionate, and sure of himself. Seeing him sitting there on my couch, blitzed on cough syrup, and in the throes of an existential crisis, I concluded that he wasn't necessarily a bad guy. He seemed pretty different from the person he played on TV. Still, I didn't want to waste the opportunity to ask about one particular thing.

"Mr. Prime Minister, since you're here, do you mind if I ask you something political?"

"Sure, though between you and me, my buddy, Berry does most of the political stuff."

"Who's Berry?" I asked.

"Did I say Berry? Fuck dude, I must be really dimed-up."

"How come you decided to go after all the doctors a couple years ago? I was in my residency at the time, and you really kind of went off on us."

"It was something about money, right?"

"Well that's what you said, but back then I was a quarter million dollars in debt and couldn't pay for groceries. It was a really bad time."

"How much of your debt did you pay off?" he asked.

"None – now I'm three hundred and six thousand dollars deep."

He shrugged apologetically. "I'm sorry, man. That sucks."

"So why did you do it?"

"It was fucking Lisa's fault."

"Who's Lisa?" I asked.

"Oh, she was this bitch I used to know in college. We went on a couple of dates, and she was all ready and set to go all the way with me, but then she got into med school, and all of a sudden she only wanted to go out with other med students. Fucking Lisa. What a whore she was."

I admit that I was quite taken aback.

"That was, um, not what I expected," I said.

"Well, you look at the heart of any major political fiasco, there's always a woman behind it. They're rotten, man – rotten right to the core. Well, I used to think that, anyway. Then I met Clara. Clara's cool."

"What about your wife?  She seems nice," I said, hoping to change the subject. I've never before wanted someone to pull out their wallet and show me photos of their children. But there I found myself, hoping for a semi-normal moment of boring, predictable conversation.

"No, she's a viper. She just wants the prestige, man. A taste of the fame."

"Come on," I said.  "No way."

"I'm telling you, man, she's poison. I know you know it, bro. You can tell just looking at her."

I started searching the room for a hidden camera. I knew I had to be on one of those French gag shows.

"Mr. Prime Minister," I said, "I don't want this to sound like I'm accusing you of being insincere, but I'm having a hard time reconciling the stuff you're saying with some of the policies you've put in place."

He stood on shaky legs and stumbled to the kitchen. He filled his cup with cooking sherry, and then collapsed back on the sofa, spilling half of it on the cushions – on my *de facto* mattress.

"I'm going to let you in on a little secret," he said. "What do you know about incels?"

Because of the late hour, and unusual circumstances of our discussion, I can only give a basic summary of what the prime minister told me.

To my surprise, he admitted that he had always had difficulty meeting girls. From his high school days, he would get into one or two-date relationships, but he revered women so much that he couldn't bring himself to be a "closer in the bedroom."

"I was putting the pussy on pedestal," he said. "I see that now."

One evening, after a night of heavy drinking, a girl in his college dorm laid the hard truth on him. Women thought he was pompous and effeminate. He spent so much time worrying that he would offend them, that he was subconsciously avoiding talking about them and was only talking about himself.

He went to seminars, and took steps towards building his confidence, but unfortunately, around that time he started hitting the cough syrup pretty hard. Women found his nervous mannerisms, combined with the dense miasmatic fog of eucalyptus and artificial grape that wreathed him, a total turn off.

He went three years without sex, and he became convinced that women only had intercourse as a way of furthering their own socio-economic agenda. He was of the belief that they were incapable of love, and that their nurturing stereotype was propagated only for the purpose of fooling men into giving them money and/or power. He began to first resent, then actually hate women on a fundamental level.

He began a controversial Reddit community for involuntarily celibate men like himself, under the pseudonym "wakeupguyz," in which men with a similar background and experience could come together and sympathize. His Reddit community festered within its echo chamber, until it was declared a hate-group six months later, and was taken offline. With no online voice, the prime minister turned to the only soapbox he could think of. He decided to run for federal politics. He knew that once united, the involuntary celibate community would be unstoppable.

A funny thing happened, however. Once he decided to run for politics, he found that women suddenly wanted him. They wanted him bad. "I was drowning in twat," he said.

To further his chances of political success he picked one woman, nearly at random, and proposed marriage. One would think that her calming presence would tame the misogynistic hate-fire that burned in his heart, but just the opposite happened. "She turned out to be a total feminoid," he said. "To her, life is a women vs men power game, twenty-four-seven. Sex is like her super weapon. I have no idea who actually fathered our children, or if they were created in some kind of laboratory to further her evil agenda."

But he played it "smart."

"I pretended to run on her agenda," he said. "I knew if I made saccharine platitudes to women, and showed a ridiculous amount of gender-biased favoritism, she, and all the she-wolf voters like her would lap it up. But what I was really doing, was the world's greatest recruitment campaign for my incel movement. By dividing the population against itself, and by further alienating the incels from mainstream society, I believed I could galvanize their movement into a true grass-roots guerrilla political powerhouse. I could be the focus of their hatred, and by sacrificing myself, I could kick start their movement. You know how alienation begets organization?"

But then, everything changed.

"I was in a dingy sports bar in Sudbury one night, basking in the ire of all the men there, when I saw this vision come walking across the room. Clara sat down at my table, and called me out on everything. It was like, an awakening. Here was this beautiful woman, making all the sense in the world, and she was sitting there, voluntarily talking with me, like I was on her level, and she had no ulterior motive. The lightbulb came on over my head. I'd been such a fool. I knew if there were one woman like Clara, there had to be others. I felt suddenly ashamed of what I had done."

"So what did you do?" I asked.

"Nothing," he said. "I realized that divisiveness could be a good thing. That we could use it to create identity groups to focus on for government spending. We devised a plan that would virtually guarantee an irreversible government gravy train of federal cash being injected into the economy. And I have to say, the results have exceeded my best expectations."

"And… you don't hate women anymore?"

"Not really. I mean, I hate my wife, don't get me wrong. And fucking Lisa. Sometimes I catch myself, but I've learned not to see them as 'women,' but as 'voters.' My job is to make sure everybody identifies as an oppressed group and then give them money. It's fun. It's like being Bob Barker."

"You know what's funny," I said, "that's the second Bob Barker reference I've been involved with this week."

Then we talked at length about *The Price is Right*, and how millennials didn't understand *Price is Right* analogies. Finally, with the PM still talking away, I fell asleep sitting up.

# 8

Relish stock (cucumbers, cabbage, water, salt, calcium chloride)
High fructose corn syrup
Distilled white vinegar
Sodium benzoate and potassium sorbate as preservatives
Guar gum
Alum
Xanthan gum
Dehydrated red bell peppers
Extractives of tumeric
FD&C Yellow #5 and Blue #1
Natural flavorings
Polysorbate 80

*So much news!* It's been a few days since I wrote.

Our grants came through. Our water-feature-turned-koi-pond is now officially an experimental indoor Asian carp farm.

The research grants also got the go ahead. With the help of Dr. Chu's resident, Emily, I wrote a white paper and submitted it. Our paper is slotted for publication in the inaugural volume of *The Canadian Women's Health Journal.* Guess which company received a twenty-seven-million-dollar federal grant for the establishment of a scientific journal dedicated to women's health?

Our company earned roughly one hundred seventy thousand dollars per hour during the three hours I spent writing a white paper.

Pay-day happened. At first it was quite disappointing. I received a two-week paycheque for two-thousand three hundred dollars. I asked Mr. Singh for a raise, prepared to vehemently argue my case. But no arguing was needed. He tripled my pay. He didn't bat an eyelid. He said, "I'm sorry,

Nicholas, I'm so used to working with millennials, I forgot you were older. Guys like us, we still care about money, don't we."

He remembered my name!

We are still the only group working out of the A.I. Women's Health Solutions office.

I saw Mahmoud again. He was eating by the experimental Asian carp farm. I walked down to speak with him, but by the time I'd exited the spiral he was gone. Clara and I plan to follow him. We think he might be up to something nefarious and exciting. I don't mean that in a racist way. We think Mahmoud is pretty cool. But he's a big mystery.

Jeff's foot has fully recovered. He spends all day every day walking the streets with Lonnie, seeding buckets and receptacles around Vancouver in preparation for the Umbreller launch. Lonnie really knows the streets. Every day at lunch, they find a bench and sit together. Jeff eats peanut butter and jam, literally licking it off cellophane, while Lonnie fires a spoonful of heroin into his arm. They're sort of an odd pairing, like Mel Gibson and Danny Glover in *Lethal Weapon*.

The environmental grants for Umbreller came through.

Lonnie moved into the apartment next door to us, which Mr. Singh co-owns with Wu Chung in a business called The So-Con (socially conscientious) Real Estate Investment Trust. They have reclassified the apartment as a homeless shelter.

Mr. Singh is gently pressuring me to certify as a physician in Vancouver. He wants me to oversee an opioid rehabilitation program out of Lonnie's apartment. Lonnie would be my only patient, but there is a five million dollar grant available for opioid rehabilitation programs in the greater Vancouver area.

"But won't that rob other rehab programs of important funding?" I asked.

"If there were other rehab programs, they would already have the funding," he said. Mr. Singh makes a good point.

•

*In other news*, the Silver Asian Carp I caught off Wu Chung's boat have gone missing. But our koi count is up by two. Clara swears she didn't steal any more koi. I am concerned our data for the department of fisheries and oceans may be corrupted. I am adjusting our study start date one week forward to account for this. I am researching the life cycles of koi fish.

Ray had a big evening and bagged forty-seven pigeons. He states he is considering live trapping them, as he feels there is only so much rock-pigeon blood one should have on one's hands.

Finally, Michael's Ritalin is concerned that he has a vocabulary confidence issue. He doesn't so much want to build his vocabulary; rather he wants to improve his confidence in the vocabulary he currently possesses. He stated that he needs a "Millennial-type solution." I believe he has come up with just the thing. He has decided to build a webpage of easily solvable crossword puzzles designed to increase linguistic confidence. All the answers in each puzzle must rhyme. Here are some of the clues:

> 4 letters – you hit it with a hammer
> 4 letters – it uses wind power to propel a boat
> 4 letters – another word for bucket
> 3 letters – old timey beer
> 5 letters – the search for the holy ______

crosswordconfidence.org has had twelve-hundred hits so far. Google analytics tells us that most hits come from Vietnam between 3am and 4am Pacific Time.

Michael's Ritalin states that he is considering enrolling in an English as a Second Language course to further boost his confidence.

# 9

*Ray and I had a* lengthy discussion about human evolution today after I caught him watching fake beheading videos at work. He stated that he wondered if watching fake-beheading videos would be adequate for triggering a mild form of PTSD, a disease, which he figured, had been capitalized into the largest subsidization scheme in the history of the civilized world. This led to a conversation about PTSD rates in civilized vs non-civilized societies, which led somehow to a discussion about Adam and Eve.

"Let's say God came down to earth today – actual God. Like there was no question he was our maker. Let's say he came down on a cloud of fire and he landed in Kelowna, and he said to the whole world, 'Look – I'm going to give you people one more chance. I'm going to deem this one apple tree the "new" forbidden tree. The rest of the world is going to be an eternal paradise – heaven on earth. Everything you can imagine, and more, will be yours for eternity. The human race will spread out across the universe and populate the distant galaxies, and you will all live forever in harmony. Just so long as nobody eats an apple from this tree.'

"How long do you think it would be before someone ate Apple 2.0?"

I thought about it. "I reckon it wouldn't be five minutes," I ventured.

"I'd guess about two," he said.

"Does that mean we've achieved the apex of intelligence?" I asked.

"I think it means we're terminal assholes."

Ray had the suspicion that Umbreller had not achieved its maximum target subsidy. He decided to list it on Liftoff Capital. He got a phone call from a company that was recruiting investment for environmentally friendly initiatives within six minutes of uploading the Umbreller profile. They offered him three hundred thousand dollars on the spot.

"They don't even want to meet?" I asked.

"No," he said.

"How much equity are they taking?" I asked.

"None."

"They're just giving you money?"

"Essentially," he said. He looked glum.

"So what's bothering you?"

"They obviously have lined up a pretty rich subsidy that I'm not aware of. Remember how much we paid Dr. Chu compared to how much we kept?  I think I'm getting rusty."

"Maybe it's private money," I suggested.

"In Canada?" He laughed. "There's no such thing."


Clara and I followed Mahmoud today at lunch. He went to Red Burrito. On the way, a Middle Eastern man, seeing his Peshawari cap, greeted him. Mahmoud seemed not to notice. He stopped at London Drugs on his way back to work, and browsed the display of PlayStation games. He noticed us watching him, and I waved. He did not wave back. Being a spy is hard.


I think the listification of all things has given us all a mild form of attention deficit disorder. I find I am unable to process information unless it is presented in list form. This would have been problematic for me if the media had assumed its current form while I was still a medical student. Textbooks would have had to adjust to compensate, using a Listverse-style narrative and chapter titles would have to be clickbait:

5 Totally Awesome Things You Didn't Know About Parkinson's Disease
10 Horrifying Signs You Might Have a Gallbladder Polyp
6 Sexy Facts About Rectal Carcinoma
The 7 Worst Things That Happen When You Ovulate
3 Crazy Tonsil Myths

Jeff and I don't watch movies anymore. Instead, we watch Cinema Sins on YouTube. That way you get to see all the things that are wrong with the movie you might have otherwise watched, and you can pretty much assimilate all the major plot points. If I had investments, I would divest myself of Mirimax.

I'm pretty sure Clara has a second apartment somewhere in our building. Yesterday she left our apartment wearing a grey sweater and returned two minutes later wearing a green sweater. I called her out on it, but she denied everything, saying it was one of those shades where you can't tell if a color is green or grey. She's an outstanding liar, because for a while I actually believed her. But then I remembered the grey sweater had a hood. The green did not. Why lie about it? Maybe she's so bathroom-shy that she rented a second apartment to poop in. That might explain it. I must remember to discuss this development with Ray.

I found the missing carp. The big silver carp that I'd spent all that effort catching off Wu Chung's boat have committed suicide. They jumped out of our water feature and into a potted palm. The crazy thing is, they all jumped into the same plant. I found them by following my nose. At first, I thought someone had deliberately murdered them and hidden them in the potted palm, but then Ray showed me a video of Asian carp jumping *en masse* when startled. I think it must have happened during one of the frenetic koi feeding sessions. We seem to have even more koi, by the way. When you feed them, it's like the water feature briefly explodes. It isn't particularly peaceful.

We are applying for a biotech grant to study the growth-promoting-effects of koi serum on healthy breast tissue. That application and study design is actually causing me to have to work, but the research grants combine in excess of two million dollars since it involves biotechnology, oceanography, invasive species, women's health issues and has post-mastectomy reconstruction ramifications.  Dr. Chu is going to be involved as well. This time we had to offer her quite a bit more money. Almost 8% of the total grant value. We decided to do it because it's a "long game kind of project," according to Mr. Singh. Ray says it's because the project is just boring enough that it's forgettable and just complicated enough that politicians won't understand it. The results don't matter so much to them as it matters to say "My government spent x amount of dollars funding women's health initiatives, and x amount of dollars studying the problem of invasive species." Once again, the message is the medium. In fact, one could argue that it's better for the politicians if the problems don't go away – that way they can keep promising to solve them.

We still have not seen anyone other than Mahmoud in the building. Since our team is stationed near the top of the spiral, I considered asking Mr. Singh if we could move our stuff from section H to section A so we wouldn't have to walk everywhere.

We put it to a vote, and all of us, myself included, voted against the move. Section H feels like home. Also, it's closer to the bathroom with the Charmin Ultra toilet paper.

Ray says he suspects the rest of the company may not factually exist. He says that when voter-blocks or target-municipalities are heavily subsidized, that it's common practice to hire employees and have them "work from home." In other words, you hire them and then split their subsidy grant with them in perpetuity.

"The subsidy grants can be quite profitable," he explained. "Remember when that Volkswagen plant opened in Ontario? The federal government pays VW something like a hundred and sixty-five grand a year per employee per year. The company doesn't have to do anything to be enormously profitable. Just take the grants and split them with the workers. Even if a car never rolls off the line, it will be a massive revenue generator for Volkswagen."

"So, we're really the only ones who work here?" I asked.

"Unless there's an audit, or a press conference, yeah."

I bought Jeff and Michael's Ritalin Costco-sized twin tub-sets of tzatziki and hummus. Jeff has lost a lot of weight and needs to buy new clothes. I can't believe I'm saying this, but I'm considering joining them in their diet. I don't care so much what I look like, but I can feel the heaviness of my body when I'm walking uphill. I also don't want to be known in our one-dimensional universe, as "the fat guy." I'd like to feel a little more springy.

Jeff used to work as a veterinarian in Halifax. I asked him why he quit his job, thinking that he had burned out on putting down poodles. "The pay was bullshit," he said. "After taxes, I couldn't pay down my student loan."

There's definitely some kind of rut happening for over-educated professionals in Canada. It's a tax-tuition-trap. They base your tuition on your expected gross earnings, without accounting for the fact that you end up paying more than half of your earnings in tax. Then they base your taxes on your gross earnings without regard to the cost of your tuition and the amount of debt you carry. You are the financial equivalent of an Amish Kid who, during Rumspringa, joins a Jim Jones-style death cult. You hand everything over to one God for the first half of your life, and then another God for the second half. Eventually it kills you. If you don't know about the grants and subsidies programs, you're basically screwed.

In our parents' generation the key to a successful retirement was hard work. In our generation the key to a successful retirement is to embrace the fact that you retired directly after high school. Time is money, after all. It helps if you're good at finding forms on government websites.

After work today, Mahmoud went to Las Tortas Gourmet Mexican Sandwiches. He took off the Peshwari cap and stuffed it into his backpack before he went inside. He hugged the girl who worked behind the counter. Clara made me wait across the street. It started to rain, and we used the Beta version of Umbreller to find an umbrella can. There were no umbrellas in it, so I checked the dumpster next to it and there were seven.

By the time I'd climbed out of the dumpster Mahmoud was gone. I followed Clara into Las Tortas.

"Hi," she smiled brightly at the woman behind the counter, "we're looking for our friend, Mahmoud. Has he been here already? We're running a little late."

"No, I don't think so."

"Great, thanks," Clara said, before placing an order.

We sat on a bench to eat our Torta Carnitas, Clara said that she believed there was more to Mahmoud than met the eye. "He may very well be at the center of a major conspiracy."

I pointed out that all of us were in fact at the very epicenter of a very major conspiracy, what with A.I. Plus Womxn's Health Solutions having been designed to bilk the government of as much tax-payer money as possible.

"That doesn't mean there isn't a second conspiracy at play," she said. "Layers upon layers."

"Like an onion," I said.

"I never thought of it that way," she said.

"What? Really?"

"No, I'm just fucking with you." She punched me in the arm.

It was a nice moment.


My mom called. She said she felt lonely so I put her on speakerphone and introduced her to Ray, Michael's Ritalin and Clara.

"You sound like lovely people," she said.

"Why don't you come out for a visit?" Jeff said. "I can pick up a cot, and you can stay in Nick's room with me." (I was now a permanent couch sleeper).

"I wouldn't want to impose," she said. Everyone made noises like that wouldn't be a problem. "Well, we'll see," she said. She sounded happy.


Lonnie disappeared. Ray thinks he's either on a smack-binge or he misses the water views from the dog park. "Lonnie's no landlubber," he explained.

"The dog park is next to False Creek, under the bridge. You can't hear the waves. All you can hear is traffic. And dogs. And people arguing about their dogs," Clara said.

"Still," Ray said.

Jeff is stuck, for the time being, placing Umbreller receptacles on his own.

# 10

Tomato purée (water, tomato paste, tomato juice)
Diced tomatoes
Rehydrated onion
Onions
Rehydrated green bell peppers
Distilled vinegar
Contains less than 2% of:
Salt
Sugar
Garlic powder
Cilantro
Lemon juice concentrate
Citric acid
Calcium chloride
Natural flavor

*Mom came to Vancouver.* Since Lonnie was gone, we put her up in apartment 406. Now, technically, I'm not proud that I made my mother live in a homeless shelter, but since there was only one occupant, and he was gone, I figured it would pass moral muster for a night or two. And did she ever spruce the place up! She washed the sheets, did the dishes, and organized Lonnie's closet. "He has some surprisingly nice suits for a homeless man," she stated.

"He's an accountant," Ray explained.

We showed her around our apartment as well. The first thing she did was tear the butcher paper off Jeff's window. "It looks like a crime scene in here," she said. "It's like the Columbine library after the massacre!"

That evening Jeff realized what the butcher paper had been for. The apartment directly across from his hosted an orgy for overweight, grey-haired men. In a way, it was encouraging to see so many people of various ethnic backgrounds come together in a colorblind celebration of their own vitality, but then the weird fat-man penises that look like wrinkled up skin tags stuck to women's pubic hair started making their presence known, and Jeff went to Costco to buy more butcher paper. "Curtains aren't going to cut it," he said.

Thankfully, Mom's window faced a different direction than Jeff's.

The koi keep multiplying. I'm working with Ray to develop optical tracking software that can recognize each individual fish by its markings. I feel like we're being tricked into working.

The other day, Mr. Singh showed up at the office with a centrifuge. "It's a gift from Wu," he said. "For the serum research. His half-sister had a lumpectomy in Hong Kong, and he says our research is very meaningful to him."

Later, on the news, there was a segment about a brazen daytime robbery. A shipping container full of expensive European lab equipment had been stolen from the shipyard. The police suspected the theft was tied to a drug ring.

Vancouver ran out of cooking sherry. Michael's Ritalin's confidence-inspiring crossword puzzle website had gone viral, and on it, he provided a link to his diet website www.healthylivingthroughcondiments.ca. "It's catching on!" he exclaimed when the manager at Whole Foods explained that there had been a run on his drink of choice.

Jeff thinks Michael's Ritalin is a genius. "Like a higher intelligence – a cyborg."

To compensate for the loss of their favorite beverage, Michael's Ritalin and Jeff have started buying pure vanilla extract. It tastes very strong, but carries an alcohol content of 35%. The first night we tried the new liquor, Ray attempted to shoot a pigeon and ended up hitting the sodium lamp that lights the rooftop patio. "That's it," he said, "we're figuring out the live traps."

We got into another discussion about our dominant

personality features. I asked Clara what her first impression of me was, and whether it still held true. "I thought of you as the scatter-brained guy who always left his briefcase behind," she said. "I still do, but now, I think you're kind of sweet too, what with your being nice to your mom and all." I was touched. I didn't mind being the scatter-brained guy.

"What was your first impression of me?" she asked.

"The mystery woman," I said. "Also, Ray told me you never poop, so that's been part of the mix all along."

She laughed. "And now?"

"The koi klepto," I said.


I don't know if it's because I've been watching so much YouTube at work, but all the story lines in my life seem to be happening in five-minute increments. Have things always happened in short increments? Has my perception of time changed such that I now break all story lines into bite-sized morsels? The answer, I think, is apparent.


We took mom out for sushi today. George Nakamoto was sitting at the table beside us. He recognized Clara and me.

"Hey! Great to see you guys!" he said, getting up and joining us at the table. "I realized after you left that I didn't get your phone number! This is so fortuitous. How are your koi working out?"

"Terrific, Mr. Nakamoto," Clara said. "How's business with you?"

"Great now that I found you! Here have some uni," he said, offering a steaming chunk of what looked like human tongue.

I thought of *Indiana Jones and the Temple of Doom*, when Indiana makes Willie Scott eat the fly-blown plate of Indian food to avoid insulting their hosts. He explains that this is more food than these people eat in a month. Mr. Nakamoto had a double chin and a pot belly. I figured he probably ate fairly well. I was weighing my options when Clara picked up a piece of uni in her chopsticks and shoved it in my mouth. The only description I can think of is "salty cream of meat."

"Delicious," I said.

"So I have some great news, guys," George said. "Your fish are in!"

"Our fish?" I asked.

"Your koi," he said. "Two hundred ninety-seven show-quality!  Along with the Kohaku, I was able to source some Taisho Sanshoku and even some Tancho. Right from Tokyo."

"That's great!" Clara said. "What do we owe you for them?"

I elbowed her a little. She put her hand on my knee and gently rubbed it to calm me down. My mother saw this and cocked an eyebrow.

"Well, I had to bring some equipment over. And with the cost of air freight, the holding aquarium and the food, we're looking at about one-twenty-five total."

"Great," Clara said. "We'll come by tomorrow. Will you take a credit card?"

The waitress brought our dinner. To my surprise, Mom joined Jeff and Michael's Ritalin in scraping off and eating the spicy mayonnaise, leaving the rest of her maki untouched.

"Mom, what are you doing?"

"Oh, you should try it honey. It's a diet I found called 'condimenting.'  I saw an ad for it on this crossword puzzle website I go to."

Jeff and Michael's Ritalin beamed.

George was a very charming man, and he spoke to my mother at length about the koi business. Like many people his age, he'd bought a house overlooking the water in West Vancouver in the early nineties, and sold it for an approximately 30000% profit. He quit his job at the phone company and decided to make his passion for koi a full-time pursuit.

"What is it you like about koi," my mother asked.

"Their orangeness, I guess," he answered. "Funny, I've never really thought about it."

He and Mom exchanged numbers, and I knew we were then resigned to buying one-hundred-twenty-five-thousand dollars' worth of decorative show-fish.

When the waiter brought our coffees, Clara's phone rang with a ringtone I hadn't heard before – Snoop Dogg and Dr. Dre's "Smoke Weed Every Day," and I couldn't help but briefly glance at the screen. The caller ID said "S.D."

"I'd better take this one," Clara said. "Can you get my dinner?  I'll get you back."

"No sweat," I said, still conscious of the place where her hand had been on my knee.

## 11

Water
Alcohol
Premium vanilla bean extractives
Sugar


*OK. I'M DRUNK.* Drunk isn't the word. I got into the vanilla extract. It's like LSD from outer space.

Here are some more crossword puzzle clues.


— You throw a penny in a well and make a _______ – 4 letters

— At Greek weddings you break a _______ – 4 letters

— Koi, trout and salmon are different kinds of _______ – 4 letters

— Living on Mt. Kailash, with parents Shiva and Parvati, this Hindu deity with the head of an elephant is one of the most worshipped in the pantheon _______ – 7 letters


Here is a list of things I know about Clara:

Favorite band – The Ramones.
Favorite Color – Green.
Does she have mysterious celebrity friends? – yes.
Does she have a secret second apartment in our building – it is suspected.
Favorite animal – dogs.
Favorite Canadian Content-driven band-success-story for band that wasn't particularly good – Our Lady Peace.
Most discussed cheesy Canadian band music video paid for with taxpayer dollars – "Life" by Our Lady Peace.
Why she finds this video is especially distasteful –

because it compares suffering from stage 4 breast cancer to the inability to master a difficult skateboard kick-flip. On top of that it strongly features Chinese script, as though it's some kind of fucking magical rune, thus inspiring a generation of feeble-minded Canadian teenagers to tattoo Chinese letters on themselves, and to trust the tattoo artist to write the correct thing.

Clara's Age when this horrendous video debuted on Much Music – 11

Does she have a tattoo of Chinese letters somewhere on her body? – Obviously.


Clara and I picked up the koi this morning. I am becoming concerned about my ability to keep our pond clean. I am, by no means, a koi pond expert. Fortunately for me, they are not picky eaters. I am considering asking to bring in a koi consultant, since the pond is at the epicenter of at least a third of our grant money.

Mr. Singh, for his part, was completely unconcerned about the cost of the new fish, and handed over the corporate card, saying, "These things pay for themselves!"

In other news, we found Lonnie. It's a bit of a story.

Wu Chung invited Michael's Ritalin over for dinner, and he extended the invitation to the rest of H-Section, as well as Jeff and my mom.

His house was one of the McMansions overlooking the water in West Point Grey. We piled out of our taxi into his roundabout driveway that was chalk-full of Bentleys, Lamborghinis, Ferraris and a fortress-like maroon Rolls Royce.

"I didn't really dress for this," I said, noting my O'Neil Grey hoodie and grungy jeans.

"What do you mean?" asked Michael's Ritalin.

"I mean that, much like the yacht party where I showed up with fishing gear, I'm arriving to a millionaire party dressed like a homeless person."

"Does it bother you?" Clara asked.

"Actually, I suppose it doesn't," I said.

"It's no big deal," Michael's Ritalin explained. "All these cars are Wu's. I think it's just us here tonight."

Ray rang the doorbell, which triggered chimes to the tune of "Sea Cruise," by Frankie Ford. Then an actual homeless man answered the door, and he was, in fact, significantly better dressed than me.

"Lonnie!" Ray pulled his friend into a bear hug. Lonnie slapped Ray on the back. Cleaned up, and wearing a Jack Victor sports coat over a purple-floral accent shirt and khakis, Lonnie looked downright posh.

"Oh my gosh, Lonnie, did you get off the smack?" I asked.

He laughed. "Not at all. In fact I just shot up."

"Well, you're looking terrific," I said.

Mom introduced herself. "Lonnie," she said, "I'm Catherine – Nicholas's mother. I'm living in your apartment."

For a second, Lonnie looked confused. Then he laughed again, "Oh – the apartment on Davie. That's great, Catherine. You can have the place, too. I just moved into a new house in Kits."

Ray stood back, looking serious. "Dude, are you crazy? A house in Kits is like two-mill minimum."

"I know," Lonnie said. "It's actually one of Wu's houses. He figured that because I'm an addict, he could use me to register it not just as a homeless shelter but also as a safe injection site. I might not be able to generate much on my own, by as a homeless addict, I'm worth a mint! And I've got a real good feeling about Umbreller. I've been putting the vibes out there, and I think it's way beyond grant worthy. Have you explored the immigration angle?"

Ray and Lonnie waffled back and forth for a minute, discussing forms and government departments.

Wu came to the door. "Lonnie, let our friends in for heaven's sake!"

Wu ushered us into the foyer. The floor was an unusual, plasticized marble.

"Thank you for having us, Mr. Chung," I said. "This is a very unusual floor."

"Thank you for noticing," he said, "it is a synthetic hockey rink."

"Brilliant!" Ray cried. "I never thought of that!"

He noticed the rest of us looking confused.

"You don't pay property tax on hockey rinks in Canada," he explained. "I never thought to go synthetic, though."

"Yes," Wu said proudly, "it is among my better accomplishments."

He knelt and kissed my mother's hand. "You must be Catherine," he said. "You are as beautiful as my own mother, God rest her soul. She, too, knew the challenges of raising a boy with autism."

Everyone looked at me.

"Me?" I asked.

"Yes," he said.

"I'm not…" I said. "I'm just shabbily dressed."

"Hmm," Wu said.

"Well, let's be honest, honey," my mother said. "You're likely somewhere on the spectrum."

"You're definitely on the spectrum," Jeff said. "Who dresses like that?"

I turned to Ray. "Dude, do you think I'm autistic?"

"It's really not for me to say," Ray said.

"I can't believe this!" I said.

"You see how you get upset?" Wu said. "It reminds me of my half-brother David."

"Was he autistic?" my mother asked.

"Very," Wu said.

"Oh, that's so hard," my mother said.

Wu took her arm and led her into the house, the issue of my autism now having been definitively settled in the absolute absence of professional medical opinion. "Do you like single malt scotch, Catherine? I have one of the best scotch bars in British Columbia."

Mom giggled.

Everyone except Ray followed them inside. He was smiling proudly at me.

"What?" I said.

He rubbed his fingers and thumb together like he was holding a full fan of cash. Then he pointed at my head.

"Remember, the preferred term is 'neurodivergent,'" he whispered.


Wu's house was eclectically appointed with archaeological artifacts that looked as though they belonged on the set of an Indiana Jones film. (If that seems like too many Indiana Jones references for one man's journal, I can assure you it isn't.) There was also a lot of high-tech gadgetry.

"This is interesting," Jeff said, fingering what looked like a touchscreen tablet mounted in the kitchen wall beside the enormous Wolf range.

"Check it out," Wu said proudly. "I enter my normal security code," he punched four numbers on the touch screen, "and it's a TV for the kitchen."

Figure skating played on the tablet, the sound coming from hidden in-wall speakers. He swiped the screen and it changed to a security feed from the front driveway. "And here is my security feed."

Wu turned it off, and went back to the code screen. "But if I enter my special code," he punched four different numbers, and there was a brief electronic whir. The panel hinged open, and two elaborate gold and enamel handguns ejected from hidden space behind the panel, their handles presented perfectly for the lucrative businessman in need of quick, stylish firepower. "Now I am ready for a gunfight."

"That's fascinating," I said.

"You would be fascinated by such a device," Wu said, closing the secret gun safe, "because of the autism."

I was going to protest but Michael's Ritalin cut in. "What are we having for dinner, Wu?"

"Oh, I got something really special for you guys," Wu said. "I think you'll be quite fond of it. But we have to wait – we have one more guest coming. A friend of yours, Ray, if I'm not mistaken."

As though on cue, the doorbell rang.

I know, for a fact, I am going to have Frankie Ford's "Sea Cruise" stuck in my head for days. Sometimes when a song gets in there, I even hear it in my dreams. Maybe I am on the spectrum. *Shit*.

Lonnie answered the door, and a familiar sinister-looking slim man with a receding hairline, narrow eyes and a grey beard ambled in.

"Doug!" Ray said, extending his hand. Douglas Coupland waved the hand away. He didn't smile.

"What the fuck, Butler?" Coupland said, his face reddening. "Arts Council grants? You hoovered up *my* arts council grants?"

"I tried to bring you in," Ray said, taking a step back. "But you were doing that blanket thing."

"That 'blanket thing' is a national fucking treasure and a statement about how history doesn't exist, regardless of whether or not it repeats itself! I didn't know you were going for the Arts Council, you greedy prick," Coupland hissed.

"We weren't. It started as a water feature, and well, one thing led to another..."

"Wait," I interjected. "There's an Arts Council grant for our koi pond?"

"It was a green-space piece that celebrates diversity," Ray said.

"How does our experimental fish farm celebrate diversity?" I asked.

"The fish are from Asia."

"Fuck that's smart," Coupland said. He was still mad, but there was obvious admiration there, too.

"Gentlemen, please," Wu said. "I didn't bring you all here to fight. I brought you here to make money. Let's have a drink, and I'll bring everyone up to speed."

"Do you have any cooking sherry, or vanilla extract?" Coupland asked. "I'm trying this new thing..." Coupland seemed to notice Clara for the first time.

"Oh, hi Clara. How are you?"

"Hi Doug." They embraced.

"You know everyone," I said to Clara.

"I was in media relations," she said, "remember?"

Coupland turned to me "Who are you?"

"He's Nicholas. He's autistic," Wu said.

"I'm not really," I said.

"Do you like bubbles?" Coupland asked.

"Bubbles?"

"You know," he went on, "when people blow bubbles, and they get carried away on the breeze, do you find it appealing?"

"Yeah, bubbles are OK, I guess."

"Great find, Wu," Coupland said. They high-fived one another.

Wu stood in the kitchen, dicing tomatoes, boiling broth and working many pots and pans. Delicious cooking smells wafted through the house while he held court, asking how things were going at A.I. Plus Womxn's Health Solutions. He seemed genuinely interested, and despite the autism discussion and the fact that I knew he was a potentially violent criminal, I found myself quite liking him.

I asked him how he came to live in Vancouver.

"That's an interesting story," he said. "I grew up in Hong Kong. I did not know my father, and my mother was a maid at the Peninsula Hong Kong. She would let me come to work with her and would put me in an empty room while she cleaned. We often saw visitors from other countries who had very nice, very rare things. I have always had a liking for rare things. When I was a boy, a man from Canada stayed as a guest at the hotel. He was making a movie about taking his wheelchair across the Great Wall of China, and was visiting Hong Kong on his way to start the journey. Normally, I would stay in my room, but that day, I wandered down to the lobby and there I met him.

"The man told me about Canada, how it was a land of opportunity for people from away. He said you could come to Canada and study in the schools there, and learn about computers. He said I could become the next billionaire, and I could apply for a government grant to support this dream. The man opened my eyes to the way of the world. When my mother passed away from bird-flu, I used what money I could scrape together to buy a one-way ticket to Vancouver."

"That's weird," Coupland said. "I didn't know you came here to study programming. How did you end up in the pharmaceutical trade?"

"I saw a hole in the market," Wu said. "It was too big to ignore. That, and I wasn't very good at programming, as it turned out."

"Mr. Chung," my brother said, "are you saying that celebrated folk hero Rick Hansen, the Man in Motion himself, inspired you to move to Canada and become a Drug Kingpin?"

"Yes," Wu said. "Mr. Hansen inspired many people. He showed the whole world that anything is possible."

Mom helped Wu finish the dinner. Wu was very polite. When they finally sat down, he began dinner by toasting her. "It is a great honor to host this wonderful woman, who has raised these two boys who are my new friends. Cheers."

We clinked glasses. Most of them were full of vanilla extract or cooking sherry.

Dinner was a style Wu called "Condiment Fusion." Bowls of everything from Mint Jelly to Bouillabaisse sauce were placed on the table and ladled into condiment-serving plates –

wide, segmented dishes that resembled porcelain Tupperware.

"Who is making these dishes?" my mother asked.

"Michael and I have been working with a manufacturer in Hong Kong," Wu said. "These are our prototypes. Do you like them?"

"They're perfect!" Mom said. "This is all so exciting!"

Dinner was delicious. At one point, Coupland turned to me. "You know, I'm curious. Forgive me if this sounds like self-interest, but I'm wondering as a person with such debilitated social skills, what do you think of my books and artwork? Do you find them relevant?"

"I read *Microserfs*," I said; "I really liked it."

Coupland scratched at his beard. "Did you relate to the characters, as so many do, as representative of your generation?"

"No, not really," I said. "I just thought it was a nice story. You know – I liked how they were all still friends in the end."

He rubbed his face, and looked exasperated. "What about *Generation X*? I've been told it's a transcendent piece."

"I didn't read it," I said. "I looked at it, but it seemed kind of boring."

"And *J-Pod*? Did you read it?"

"Yes, I did read that one. Someone left it on an airplane."

"And?"

"I thought it was weird that you made yourself a character in it. Like you think your work is so important that you're this cornerstone of counterculture."

"That's very rude," he said. "One of my characters in *J-Pod* was based on Wu. Did you at least like him?"

"I'm sorry," I said. "I don't really remember the characters. I thought you made them forgettable on purpose."

Coupland made a harrumphing sound. "How about my art? Did you know I once chewed up and spit out two of my past books and turned the pulp into a wasp nest to signify that we are a world without history?"

"If we're a world without history, why are you telling me about it?" I said.

"Hmm. How about 'Towers,' where I built towers out of LEGO?" He showed me a picture on his phone.

"Well LEGO is fun," I said, "but even before I knew all about these grants and subsidies, I could see through that one as the easiest possible way to take government money."

His cheeks flushed, and he turned to Ray. "What about you, Butler? Do you see the deeper meaning?"

"Honestly?" Ray asked.

"Yes, honestly," Coupland said.

"I'm going to have to agree with Rain Man over there," he gestured at me. "It's pretty obvious, dude."

Coupland sat quietly for a moment. "Shit," he said finally. "I need to get ahead of this."

"How about this," Ray said. "We build a website called www.dissingdoug.com. We get you a grant and call it a multi-media exhibit. In it, all we do is ask Nick, here, to write honest reviews of your books and your other art exhibits. That way, you take ownership of the criticism. Call the whole thing 'Doug Takes it on the Chin,' or some shit like that."

"You can find the grant money?"

"No problem," Ray said. "We'll split it three ways – 30 to Nick, 30 to me, and 40 to you."

"No chance, Butler," he said.

"Fine, you navigate the federal and provincial websites, find the paperwork, fill it out and mail it. Your choice."

"Goddamn it," Coupland swore. "You got yourselves a deal."

We shook on it and www.dissingdoug.com was born.

After some time, Wu served desert bowls of maple syrup, and he got down to business.

"How is the experiment with the koi going?" he asked.

"Which experiment?" Ray said. "The Women's Health one, or the Fisheries and Oceans one?"

"Fisheries," Wu said. He had a sudden laser-like focus.

Ray turned to me. "So far so good," I said. "To be honest,

I'm not sure what it is we're out to prove. Our koi pond is in the atrium of a building on Cambie Street. I am pretty certain that there's no conceivable way it will have an effect on the Pacific Salmon fishery."

Wu smiled.

"What?" I asked.

"Could everyone please follow me?" he said.

Wu led us out to his patio and then down a footpath through his expansive, partly forested backyard. I could hear running water, and as we wound out of the decorative palms, we came upon an elaborate man-made pond with a trickling waterfall.

Wu opened an app on his phone, and soft lighting glowed from the trees and false stones around us.

In the distance, the lights of Pacific freighters in English Bay twinkled like zirconium, brilliant and full of secrets.

"This is beautiful!" Clara said.

"Thank you," Wu said. "I built this pond, inspired by the work you are doing with Ravi Singh."

I examined the pond and saw it was full of marbled orange and white koi.

"The other night, when you were fishing from my boat, I thought you might be a little bit strange," he said to me. "But when I heard what happened to the silver carp in your pond, I became very curious indeed. So curious, in fact, that I devised this experiment." He gestured toward his koi pond.

"You went fishing off his yacht?" Coupland chortled. "Classic."

"Lonnie," Wu said, "can you fetch the bucket over there beside the pool house."

"Sure thing, Mr. Chung," Lonnie said.

Lonnie wrestled a large blue pail from the pool house to the edge of the koi pond where we stood.

"If you will?" Wu said, shining the light from his phone into the bucket. We gathered round. Two large silver carp swam round and round in lazy circles.

Wu tipped them into his koi pond and they darted away toward the waterfall.

Wu held up a hand, to signify that we should remain where we were, then turned and walked briskly back to the path. He grunted, and I turned to see him swivel-walking a heavy potted palm across the lawn to the edge of the pond.

He produced a baggie of pellets from the inner pocket of his sports coat – fish food, I knew from experience.

"Observe," he said.

He tossed the fish food into the pond and the surface immediately fractured into a roiling feeding frenzy. This went on for five seconds or so before there was a loud THUMP and Clara screamed. The potted palm shook. A second later, another thump followed and the palm shook again.

"What in the fuck?" Ray said to himself.

Wu, smiling, shone his light into the base of the potted palm. The two silver carp lay in the moss and soil, their gills flared, their mouths gawping.

"No way," said Coupland.

Nonchalantly, Wu bent down and hoisted the carp, one at a time, back into his koi pond. Once again he threw in a fistful of pellets, and this time while we watched, after only a fraction of a second, both silver fish exploded from the surface, landing square in the potted palm base.

Wu turned to Ray. "How much do you think it would be worth to the Canadian government, if we could solve the Asian carp crisis?"

"Holy shit," said Ray.

Wu turned to Coupland. "How much grant money do you think you could generate by turning English Bay into a koi pond, as an environmentally friendly living sculpture?

"Holy shit," Coupland said. "We're rich!"

"Indeed, it would seem so," Wu said.

**12**

Tomato purée (water, tomato paste)
Vegetable oil (contains one or more of the following: soybean oil, corn oil)
High fructose corn syrup
Salt
Dried onions
Extra virgin olive oil
Romano cheese (cow's milk, cheese cultures, salt, enzymes)
Spices
Natural flavor


Excerpt from www.dissingdoug.com

*A Review of Digital Orca Sculpture*

Digital Orca Sculpture is a sculpture of a killer whale, which appears to be pixelated, and was produced by self-appointed-zeitgeist-counterculture-superhero Douglas Coupland.

The sculpture does indeed look like a pixelated killer whale, so in that respect it has achieved its purpose. Presumably it is a commentary on the digitalization of a modern age. Or maybe it's supposed to be Coupland raging poetically against a generation of Canadians who observe the world through the screen on their phone. What I suspect, however, is that because it is built out of LEGO – like blocks, its main purpose was to be easily assembled, and quickly installed, and thereby be extremely profitable for "the artist." At the time of its creation there were two separate Canada Council for the Arts grants available – one titled "Nature in Art," and the other titled "Technology in Art."

Personally, I would rather see someone with actual sculpting skills make a statue that looks like an actual killer whale, but my suspicion is that art school no longer has any connection to artistic skill, since the concept of being "cutting edge," has been promoted to alleviate the modern Canadian artist of the burden of learning art. Now they call it "design." Because Coupland has successfully promoted himself as a "national treasure," he, of course, was awarded both grants. Hence we have "Digital Orca Sculpture."

*I WENT TO SEE A PSYCHIATRIST.* Since I didn't have a referral, I paid out of pocket. The fact that I'm including this detail says just about everything about why I went to see her.

Dr. Suma asked me to perform a few tests. She did a fifteen-minute interview, and then sat quietly writing notes. When she finally looked up and smiled, I asked, "So how'd I do?"

"Pretty good," she said. "I suspect you have a pretty mild form of what, until recently, we called Asperger's. You seem to be functioning quite well, all things considered. I don't think you need a prescription."

"You're shitting me," I said. "People with Asperger's are supposed to dislike changes in routine. My whole life has been flipped upside down these past few months, and I'm fine with it."

"Hmm," she said. "See, in this case, you controlled your decision. Have you ever found yourself in a rage, screaming at the news, because events you cannot control have changed your life significantly?"

I didn't answer.

"OK, tell me this – do you like bubbles?"

•

I've decided I'm OK with being on the spectrum – neurodivergent, I'm apparently supposed to call it (which kind of sounds like the origin of a superhero story). In fact, it makes it easier to digest a lot of the parts of life I've always found mysterious. Why did I used to get so much more upset at the political news on television than everyone else? Why am I perpetually single and incapable of asking women on dates? Why, when I'm hugged by someone, can I only wonder how many germs they are breathing on me? Now I have an answer. Neurodivergence. It's kind of liberating. I can just shrug and say "Mild neurodivergence," and not worry about the problem.


I told Ray about my visit to the psychiatrist. "Great," he said. "Did you get it in writing?"

I showed him the doctor's note. He got busy applying for an employment grant on my behalf. It's for an extra twenty-thousand dollars per year. He even got Mr. Singh to agree to let me keep it all, since we're generating so many research grants.

Speaking of research, Dr. Chu's resident, Emily, came by the office today. She wore the dazed and frazzled look I remember from residency. It's the look that says, "I was up all night, I'm supposed to work all day, I have to get my research project done, and my board exams are less than two years away." Residency is just plain shitty. I didn't tell her that she smelled a bit like B.O. I've been there.

I introduced myself and offered to help extract the koi serum. It took us a few hours of googling to figure out the most humane way to bleed a koi fish, and then we chose a few unfortunate animals and needled them. It's funny how little blood you get from a Japanese show fish. We had to be careful not to kill them, since we had a grant application in process centered on ethical animal-centric research.

In total, we only pulled off about ten milliliters of blood, and we spun that down in our centrifuge to four milliliters of plasma.

"It's a start," Emily said.

She left with the serum, without so much as a goodbye.


I told Clara about the psychiatrist. "Do *you* think you have Asperger's?" she asked.

"Maybe," I said. "It explains some things."

"Come with me," she said.

We left work and walked to the dog park on the other side of the Cambie Street Bridge, where Lonnie used to sleep. I had to keep hiking at my pants. They had either stretched, or I was starting to lose weight from all the walking. The sun was brilliant. There was too much blue. Blue was everywhere.

"Do you think they made all the buildings blue to make up for the fact that the sky is usually grey here?" I asked.

She thought about it. "That's a good question," she said. "Kind of like an inverse city, where the ground is blue and the sky is grey."

I nodded.

"There's a lot of stuff happening inside that head of yours, isn't there," she said.

"You think I really do have Asperger's, don't you?"

"A lot of bright people do," she said.

"You think I'm bright?" I asked.

"Very," she said.

She may as well have kissed me. It's amazing how far a little kindness goes.


At the dog park, we sat on a bench and watched the spaniels and dachshunds and miniature rottweilers.

"Do you like dogs?" she asked.

"Sure. Yeah. We had dogs when I was a kid."

"How come you don't have one now?" she asked.

"My dad got sick, and I guess it was just too much work. I was back and forth a lot, and I wouldn't know what to do with a dog."

"Ah, here we go," she said. A pretty, fashionable brunette woman had just walked into the park with a brown and white piebald Jack Russell that jumped and pulled at its leash, and acted like it had just free-based an ounce or two of cocaine.

"Excuse me," Clara said, "that's a beautiful dog!"

"Oh thanks!" the woman said.

Clara squatted down to pat it and motioned for me to do the same. "What's his name," she asked?

While they talked about the Jack Russell, I found myself lost in the act of petting it. The dog licked my forearm while I ran my fingers down its back, over its head and across its velveteen ears.

When Clara stood, I followed her lead, smiling at the woman, but I was a little disappointed. It was nice, petting the dog.

"How was that?" Clara asked.

"Great," I said. "You know, I didn't realize how much I missed having a dog until today. Funny how you don't think about these things."

She put her hand on my cheek and turned my face so I was looking into her eyes. "You're a beautiful man," she said. "I think you should know that."

I was embarrassed and tried to turn away, but she held me there.

"I'm..." I didn't know what to say. I wanted to tell her she was beautiful too, but the words wouldn't come.

"You're a good person," she said, "but you should be more confident."

She ran her fingers through my hair. "I like that you live in your own head. Your head seems like an interesting place to live."

"It is," I said. "You should come for dinner sometime."

She laughed and the moment passed. My heart didn't stop pounding until we were back at the office.


Excerpt from www.dissingdoug.com

*A Review of "Marilyn," by Douglas Coupland*

"Marilyn" is basically an image of Marilyn Monroe done in bright, garish colors to express to the viewer how contemporary and punk the artist is. Then there's some black stuff dripping from her hair, down her forehead. Stephen King would call it "ichor." And on top of that, her eyeballs are dripping red paint. Like Coupland is saying, "Look at me, I've invented the concept that superficial beauty can hide an ugliness within." It's like he's never seen a TV show and thinks he's discovered an enormous secret about the nature of mankind.

I will hand it to him, the background has a floral, paisley pattern evocative of 70's wallpaper that's quite nice. He should have just left it at the wallpaper. Maybe there is something to this "design" stuff.

The painting, on the whole, is unoriginal and may as well have been the cover for a biography of the Sex Pistols.

You want to be bold, Coupland, I suggest you swap Marilyn for someone other than an attractive blonde woman: perhaps a one-eyed Inuit lesbian amputee with a prison tattoo on her face. Try to find a grant for the message "anybody can be an asshole."  Or "Sometimes you're as fucked up as you look." Three words – need not apply.


Wu Chung, Mr. Singh and Doug Coupland all came by A.I. Plus Womxn's Health Solutions this afternoon. They used one of the conference rooms and brought Ray into their meeting.

They are working on the koi project. Ray was using his laptop and looking up grants and subsidies while Mr. Singh wrote them down on the whiteboard.

After the meeting, Ray locked himself inside the conference room and wouldn't come out. I knocked on the door.

"I'm subsidizing!" he said. "It's going to take a while!"

He didn't come home with us this evening.


Michael's Ritalin and I set the new pigeon live-traps on the roof. I asked him how the condimenting thing was going.

"The take up has been extraordinary!" he said. But he didn't sound as perky as usual.

"What's wrong?" I asked.

"Well, it turns out that a few other people are writing books about condimenting as well. My agent called to let me know. It's like everyone thinks they've invented it."

"How's the book coming?" I asked.

"Oh, it's maybe halfway there," he said. "Here, I'll send you the Word file." He used his phone to send me an email file.

I opened the file after everyone went to bed. His half-finished book was four-hundred pages long. The first twenty pages were filled with some of the most touching poetry I have ever read. I openly wept, just reading the forward. The first chapter was titled "Condimenting: A New Way of Life." It described, in iambic pentameter, a child walking in the snow, excited and alone for the first time, feeling the squeak and crunch of the stuff under his boots. The reader, of course, knows that the child is in grave danger, but the boy is full of Buddhist wonder and curiosity. I've never read anything like it. At the end of the chapter is a recipe for homemade organic plum sauce.

# 13

Tomatoes (contain tomato juice, citric acid, calcium chloride)
Water
Dehydrated onion
Coconut milk (contains water, sulfites)
Butter ghee
Tomato paste
Garlic
Ginger purée (contains canola oil, citric acid, potassium sorbate)
Salt
Sugar
Spices (contain cayenne pepper)
Cilantro
Modified corn starch
Potassium sorbate
Natural flavor
Citric acid
Rosemary extract
Calcium disodium EDTA

Excerpt from www.dissingdoug.com

*A Review of "Gumhead"*

OK, Gumhead is a funny concept. It's a big statue of Coupland's head and you're allowed to stick gum to it. I like the name. But here's the thing. He used his own fucking head. Now maybe he used his own head because he didn't want to offend anyone else. But I suspect he used his own head because gumball by gumball he wants to cement his place as the darling of the Canadian art scene and by doing so, become a favorite for future grants and endowments.

I would have used William Shatner's head. Not only would it be recognizable, but it would have the funny effect of playing out like an episode of *Star Trek* in which Captain Kirk is attacked by the Sticky Spitters of Juicy Fruit 8.

Anyway, A+ for amusing concept. C- for execution. Dammit, Coupland, just let other people decide if you're relevant!


Frances McCain, the homeless economist-slash-journalist, finally made his debut appearance at A.I. Plus Womxn's Health Solutions.

We had gotten greedy with the Arts Council thing. Since the Koi Pond was officially registered as a public work of art, it meant that the front door had to be left unlocked.

We arrived this morning to find a disheveled, unshorn man in a rumpled pinstripe suit sleeping on the floor beside the water feature.

"Hi," Clara said. "Can we help you?"

He woke up and stretched. Still sitting on the floor, he began to scowl at us. "Frances McCain, the Free Press," he said. "I have some goddamned questions that need answering."

"Hi Frances," Michael's Ritalin said. "You look like you could use a coffee."

"Hmm," Frances said. "I suppose I could use a coffee."

"Come on upstairs," Clara said. "Are you hungry?"

She set Frances up with a coffee in our conference room, and then she and I went out to buy donuts. I had no idea where to get a donut in Vancouver. I had never seen anyone eat a donut within city limits.

"Hey," I said once we were out of earshot, "when you thought I was Frances, you were much more stand-offish."

"When I thought you were him, I thought he'd broken into our apartment, remember?"

"Oh yeah," I said.

We entered a place called "Cartem's Donuts." There was a glass display case featuring scores of delicious-looking specimens.

"What kind of donut do you think Frances would like?"

"I don't know," I said. "If it were me, I'd get something weird looking. Maybe the London Fog?"

"Let's be safe," she said. She ordered six Vanilla Bean and six London Fog donuts.

"Why get a dozen?" I asked.

"Because that's how you buy donuts," she said.

"But why do we do that?"

She locked eyes with me and held them there. "Such an interesting place, that brain of yours," she mused, then turned to the server.

"Excuse me, I've changed my mind. We'll have seven of each."

She turned to face me. "So long as I live, I'll never order an even dozen of anything again."

"What if it's prepackaged?"

"I'll open the package and take one out. Deal?"

We shook on it.


Back at the office, Frances was taking an inventory. It seemed like he was counting the number of desks, chairs and computers. Clara presented him with the donuts.

He didn't thank her, he just tucked in, stuffing a Vanilla Bean into his mouth. He looked like he hadn't eaten in a month.

Smacking loudly, he asked "Where is everyone? It says in my paperwork that A.I. Women's Health Solutions employs over one hundred recently immigrated Canadians. And yet I've only seen three of you all morning."

Ray came out of his conference room and waved good morning. "OK, four of you," Frances went on. And forgive me for saying, but you don't look as if you're exactly fresh off the boat." He grabbed another donut and bit it. Whipped-cream filling plopped on his suit androlled down the rumpled lapel.

"They're on Ukraine time," Ray said. "A lot of them work from home unless there's a deadline coming up."

Ray made to shake hands with Frances, but Frances thought he was trying to steal the donut. He hunched back and growled. I was transported to the movie theater in New Brunswick where I first met Gollum from *Lord of the Rings*.

"Whoa, take it easy," Ray said.

"Take it easy, take it easy," Frances mocked. "That's all you people do is take it easy. At the end of the day, someone else's hard work paid for all this, so people like you can take it easy. No thank you, I say. I will not 'take it easy.' Furthermore, why in the hell is the floor uneven? Some kind of tax-payer-funded shenanigans, I'm sure."

"Really, Frances," Clara said, "you're going to give your-self a stroke. Why don't you sit and watch the koi for a while. Many people swear by it. They say a koi pond can cure hyper-tension. Besides, Ray here has been working all night. I don't think it's very fair to call him lazy, the way you just implied. Further, we've grown accustomed to our spiral workplace and we consider it a second home. Would you go into someone's house and insult his or her floorplan? It's kind of rude."

Frances, who was clearly not used to being spoken to in this way, responded the way a grade school child would to a stern teacher.

"I'm... I'm sorry Ray. I'm sorry for insulting the floor... plan, uh..."

"Clara," she said.

"Sorry, Clara."

"Good," Clara said. "Now I'm going to show you the koi pond. You can meet my favorite fish. I call him 'Mr. Chubby.'"

"Because he's fat?" Frances asked, seemingly mesmerized by Clara's voice.

"No, it's because he looks like a dildo I used to have in college called Mr. Chubby," Clara said.

We all stared. "I'm kidding," she said, "he's fat. Come on, let's go."

Frances allowed Clara to lead him down the spiral to the koi pond.

When they were gone, I turned to Ray.

"What do we do?" I asked.

"Hopefully she'll get the backstory and we can figure it out from there."


From our place in the spiral, we watched Clara speaking to Frances while he ate donuts and examined the koi. At one point, Mahmoud came in the front door, saw the two sitting by the water feature, and turned around and left.

"Damn," I said. "I've been waiting for him to come back."

"How come?" Michael's Ritalin asked.

"I must learn his secrets," I said.

"That's kind of weird."

"I'm mildly neurodivergent."

Michael's Ritalin nodded his understanding.

"What did you think of the diet book?" he asked.

"It's transcendent," I said. "Where did you learn to write like that?"

"In my English as a Second Language course. I feel like the addition of poetic fiction really helps the recipes come alive."

"Unbelievable."


Clara took a phone call and hustled out of the building at three o'clock leaving a dazed Frances by the koi pond.

Not knowing what else to do I offered to take him out for sushi. We met Jeff at The Eatery. "Where's Mom?" I asked. I'd assumed she would be joining us.

"She went to Tokyo with Wu," he said. "Wu says he thinks of her as a surrogate Canadian mother. He wanted to give her a vacation, since he never got a chance to show the world to his real mother."

"Does she know he sells, uh…" I eyed Frances, not wanting to raise alarm bells, and when I saw he was looking at the menu, I mimicked shooting a syringe full of drugs into my arm.

"Yeah, she does," Jeff said. "She says she wants to take him to church. She said she thinks of it as addressing the opioid crisis head-on by affecting change from the inside."

I introduced Jeff and Frances.

"Do you work with Clara as well?" Frances asked. He was smitten.

"No, we're friends. I'm in the tech sector. I used to be a veterinarian. But you know how things change."

"Uh huh," Frances nodded.

He ordered seven sushi rolls, and just like with the donuts, he ate voraciously. Jeff had a bowl of "sushi toppings," which included roe and spicy mayonnaise and avocado paste – The Eatery was "condiment friendly."

Near the end of the meal, Frances suddenly looked up, seemingly embarrassed. "Oh, gosh guys – uh I don't have any money to pay for this."

"It's OK, I've got it," I said.

"You guys aren't bad, you know?" he said. "Not at all what I expected."

He continued stuffing his face.


Not knowing what to do with our somewhat surly, homeless economist-cum-journalist, Jeff and I invited him to stay in Mom's (formerly Lonnie's) apartment. I explained this situation to Michael's Ritalin and Ray, as we carried live traps full of flapping and cooing city pigeons down the stairwell, and loaded them into the back of a Ford Fusion Ray had rented.

Ray thought it probably wasn't a bad idea to keep Frances close, but he warned us not to trust him. "If he gets a sniff of how deep our system goes before we turn him, there's going to be hell to pay."

He was about to roll up his window to drive away when I asked, "Hey man, what are you going to do with those birds?"

"For now, it's better if you don't know," he said.


Umbreller got airtime today!  National CBC Radio hostess Anna Maria Tremonte interviewed Jeff and Michael's Ritalin about the concept. They played up the environmental angle and Jeff got three emails offering government funding before a buyout offer came in from the city of Toronto for five million dollars. Ray told them to hold off on selling out, and instead, offer to license the app to any cities that want it for $500k per year until the right offer comes along. "You'll get at least twice that," Ray said.

"We don't have any users yet," Michael's Ritalin argued.

"You don't need them. You just need to virtue signal harder. Here, look."

Ray showed an ad on the screen of his laptop. One half of the page was a landfill littered with broken umbrellas. The other half was a green field and blue sky. The banner simply said "Umbreller."

"Mind if I post it?" He asked.

"Sure," Jeff said.

Ten minutes later they had a buyout offer for eight million. "It's worth at least ten times that much in municipal grants over the next five years," Ray explained. "That's why they want it."


Mom called from Tokyo. "Nick, is Jeff there?" she asked.

"No, he's out working on Umbreller. They had some big buyout offers today."

"Well do me a favor," she said. "Try to figure out how he would feel about having an adopted brother?"

"What?"

"Wu wants me to adopt him. I think it's a great idea. It's just symbolic of course, but this man needs a mother figure."

I couldn't process this so I changed the subject. "How's Tokyo, Mom?"

"Expensive," she said. "They have grapes here that are the size of apples, but they cost something like a thousand dollars."

"That's nice," I said. "Is it like the Bill Murray movie?"

"Yes, it's exactly like that."

"When are you coming home?"

"I don't know," she said. "Wu has business here. I suppose I'll come home when he's finished."

"Love you, Mom."

"I love you too."

At the office today, Ray, Mr. Singh, Clara, and Michael's Ritalin brought a cake and sang happy birthday to me. I'd forgotten my own birthday!  Not only that but Ray gave me a present from all of them. It was wrapped in bubble wrap, with a big red bow.

Can you guess what they gave me?

Actually, I can't play those games. They gave me sneakers. They were simple black and white ones with a shiny toe cap. "They're Lanvins," Ray explained. "A perfect starter sneaker for the budding grantrepreneur."

"I don't know what to say," I said. "I'm touched."  I *was* touched, too. My eyes had welled up so my friends looked like blurry videos of themselves.

•

Coupland called. He was pissed off about something I wrote about one of his sculptures on www.dissingdoug.com.

"It sounds like you're having a really visceral reaction to the piece," I said. "The purpose of the art has been achieved."

"You're not an artist," he said. "You're a critic. One who doesn't know anything about art!"

"I know a visceral response when I hear one," I said.

"Fuck. You're right," he said. "Shit." Then he hung up.

Mahmoud came to the office late in the afternoon. He was looking for Mr. Singh, but Mr. Singh had already left.

Before leaving I took a bathroom break and peaked into the boardroom Ray had been working in the other day. The white boards that ran around the room had an itemized list of 57 departmental grants.

When we got home, Ray went to see Frances but he didn't answer the door. "Uh oh," Ray said.

We went online to find his blog and found an article written with today's date. It was titled "A.I. Plus Womxn's Health Solutions: Technology meets Medicine, or Taxpayer Funded Tomfoolery?"

The article had ten views. In it, Frances described the koi pond, the mostly absent workforce, and the spiraling office structure. He described three of the grants our office used (though thankfully he only detailed a few of the smaller employment grants and none of the larger research ones). He did write a very kind review of the staff he had met, even going so far as to describe Ray as a "good old-fashioned hard worker."

Frances promised to keep investigating.

The article that preceded this one was titled "Hide and Go Sleep: A Guide to Vancouver's Best Hedgerows and Park Benches for the Unemployable Modern Conservative."

That article had two thousand views.

"This isn't a complete disaster," Ray said. "But I think we'd better find him."

"What do we do when we find him?" I asked.

"Well, we can either kill him or give him a job."

Using his article as a guide we found Frances setting up camp in a hedgerow that ran along the community garden outside St. Paul's Hospital.

"You don't have to sleep outside, Frances," Ray said. "Come on back and stay with us."

"I can't do that," Frances said. "It could compromise my journalistic integrity. I wrote the article you know. You can't buy me with a bed and a meal." He jutted out his jaw.

"Don't worry about that," Ray said. "We can't let you sleep outside."

"Don't try to silence me," Frances said. "I know all about your last company, Grant Connections. I know who bought it and why."

"That's not a secret, and I'm not trying to silence you," Ray said. "Now come on. We want to talk to you about a job."

In the end, Ray got ahold of Mr. Singh and confirmed we could give Frances a position at A.I. Plus Womxn's Health Solutions. His title would be "Research Coordinator," and his duties would include managing the salinity and pH of the koi pond. Frances seemed genuinely enthusiastic to have a job. I let him borrow some clothes for his first day.

Tonight I asked Ray where he had found the money to hire Frances.

"It's company money. He doesn't qualify for anything that I can see."

"That must be killing you," I said.

"Yup."

"He's homeless and mentally unstable," I said. "That help?"

"It could if he were depressed or suffered from certain triggers – red hats, confederate flags, that kind of thing. I'll come up with something."

That got me thinking.

"Hey, why did the company hire us? Are we subsidized?"

"Yes, I'm sure we all are" Ray said.

"For what?"

"In my case, I'm one quarter Cree."

"Get out of town," I said. "What about me?"

"It would have been something from your resume or your application," he said.

I thought about it. In the application there had been the standard section about mental health. Normally, I just lied on that part, but this time I'd checked off "depression."

"What about Clara and Michael's Ritalin?"

"Clara, I have no idea. Michael's been to prison though. He presumably got an ex-convict resettlement subsidy."

"Fuck off," I said. "Really?"

"Oh yeah," Ray said. "I'm surprised he's never mentioned it to you."

Excerpt from www.dissingdoug.com

*A Review of Four Seasons*

"Four Seasons" is classic Coupland. Public funding? Check. Bright Colors? Check. Easily assembled modular design to be cost effective? Check.

The oversized multicolored cones that make up "Four Seasons" aren't so much an eyesore as they are a disruption of the landscape. That in itself wouldn't be so bad, but the fact that Coupland explains that the colors were chosen from the palette of the Laurentian Pencil Crayon Company, in order to appeal to the school-days nostalgia of Canadians and to further cement his existence as the Gord Downey of art in our country is annoying and over the top. Years ago, a man named Nelson Bunker Hunt tried (and failed) to corner the silver market. I feel like Coupland is trying to corner the Canadian public art market.

## 14

*MICHAEL'S RITALIN GOT* a buyout offer for crosswordconfidence. org from *The New York Times*. He asked Ray and I for advice. "They say nobody wants to spend the time trying to solve their puzzles anymore," he explained. "They said the only way to tap the millennial market is with instantly solvable puzzles, and I was the first to market."

"What I can't reconcile," I said, "is how you could have possibly had any vocabulary confidence issues and yet written 'The Condiment Diet.' It's a poetic masterpiece!"

"Well, I picked up a lot in my ESL class," he said. "Those classes really put the public school system to shame."

After an afternoon of rooftop contemplation, he decided to sell crosswordconfidence.org for seven hundred fifty thousand dollars. We opened a bottle of carbonated vanilla extract to celebrate, and co-created a goodbye puzzle. Here are some of the clues:

1)  Many people sit on them (plural) – 6 letters

2)  To go from one floor of the house to another you must use them – 6 letters

3)  These stand up on the back of your neck when you are spooked – 5 letters

4)  Hayseed towns and counties host them every summer. They feature pie eating contests, prize pigs, and country bumpkin teenagers falling in love (plural) – 5 letters

5)  When a stranger keeps looking at you with an unbroken gaze, and it makes you uncomfortable you could say that he _______ at you. – 6 letters

"We still have Umbreller," he said. "I can focus on that. Well, that and my real job."

In other Michael news, with Wu gone, he has run out of

Ritalin. So now he is just Michael again. In truth, he is more like "Michael's Brain in need of Ritalin," but that's too long to write so for now he's Michael. It turns out he never had a prescription for Ritalin. Wu was simply sharing his own private supply.

"He puts it in a little brown prescription bottle with my name on it so I don't get arrested," Michael said, wistfully. "I miss Wu."

Michael still speaks in a chipper upbeat voice, but you get the sense that he's dying inside. I would have thought the crossword money would help. "Money doesn't solve problems," Michael explained cheerily. "Ritalin solves problems."

We made him a doctor's appointment.

Clara and I have been going to the dog park on the regular. I find petting dogs soothing, and she likes going for walks. She confided that she does indeed have a separate apartment in our building.

"Why don't you stay in it? Why do you stay with us?" I asked.

"Why do you think?"

I couldn't think of an answer.

She said she'd show it to me sometime, but made me promise to keep her secret.

Mom called again. She's in Hong Kong now. Wu is working with a biology lab there, and she is exploring Kowloon. "What's it like?" I asked.

"Fucking humid."

We saw a car accident this morning on our way to A.I. Plus Womxn's Health Solutions. A Ferrari La Ferrari with a novice sticker jumped the curb and plowed into a Mercedes.

The Ferrari driver walked away from the wreck, but the Mercedes driver appeared to be stuck. Lithium smoke billowed from the Ferrari's battery pack, and Ray sprang into action, using his pocketknife to cut the Mercedes driver free. He pulled the man, semi-conscious, from the wreck through the smashed driver's-side window and laid him on the sidewalk. We were all surprised to see the injured man was television superstar Michael C. Hall, of *Six Feet Under* and *Dexter* fame. He was very pleasant once he came around. He thanked Ray profusely. Ray seemed mildly embarrassed.

We haven't seen Frances or Mahmoud in days. The koi appear to be healthy so I can only assume that Frances is managing the pond.

Coupland released a new novel called *Zeronia*. The first three pages are sequential prime numbers. I haven't gotten any further than that.


I finished reading Michael's half-manuscript. Chapter 7, in which the writer which compares the death of a forget-me-not to the 1941 Battle of Crete, and follows that with a recipe for non-dairy tzatziki, is heart wrenching.


I asked Michael about prison. "Oh," he said, "it was one of those crazy real estate things."

"I need details, Michael," I said. "I used to watch *Law and Order* obsessively."

"Well OK," he said, "but I need some extract first." He put away his Tinder feed and let me pour him a glass of the vanilla.

"This was a few years ago, during the big Chinese boom. I was just getting my feet wet with REMAX when the real estate market exploded. My first listing was for a single storey detached in Kits. They listed at four-seventy-five, which was average for their neighborhood and square footage. The first offer came in for four-sixty-five, then came a second, third and fourth offer. Three overseas offers came and there was a ten-way bidding war. The house ended up selling for two-point-three million. I cleared over a hundred thousand dollars on my first listing. It was bananas!

"I wanted a strong follow-up, but with the sudden influx of Asian money, all the buyers wanted to use Asian sounding agents, and so all the sellers wanted to use the same. There was this stock photo that was circulated on every news network in the world whenever a story about the Vancouver real estate bubble made the news – it was a For Sale sign with the agent name "Spice Lucks," and her phone number. The implication was that Asians were cornering our market, and agents with names like Spice Lucks were corrupting the city, et cetera, et cetera.

"Now I did my research and found out that Spice Lucks had died two years before. Quickly, I called the phone company and switched my number to hers, from the stock photo.

"Then the calls started coming in. Every time I saw a foreign exchange, I would answer the phone 'Spice here.'

"I was rolling in it. All I had to do was pretend to be Spice Lucks, and then later when we did the paperwork, I would explain that Spice was just my business name, if the clients ever noticed.

"The problem was, the other agents noticed. Someone called me in. I got busted for pretending to be Spice. Technically it wasn't fraud – I didn't sign her name on any of the paperwork or anything. But they called it 'attempted fraud.'

"I did six months in Fraser Regional. I had my license suspended for another six months. I was fined by the CREA for half my profits, and ended up stuck with money tied into a few North Van homes and no way to sell them. They were tough times.

"But in a way, it all worked out. Jail wasn't so bad. It was embarrassing, but I met lots of other real estate agents, and I took a business course. It was kind of like a real-life LinkedIn. Plus, I qualified for a Convict Rehabilitation Subsidy so it made it a lot easier to find work after the bubble popped."

"Weren't there murderers and rapists in the prison?" I asked.

"Sure, but there were about twenty real estate agents for each one of them. Nobody fucked with us."

"Are you saying you were in a prison gang specifically limited to real estate agents? This… sounds like a Will Ferrell movie."

He laughed. "It wasn't that formal. We just had one another's backs. I'll tell you what, prison would make a terrific corporate team-building exercise.

"Sidenote, have you ever noticed that Will Ferrell and Doug Coupland look like they could be brothers?"

I thought about it. "I think it's the eyes. They're kind of… baleful."

"Now that's a word you see in print but almost never hear in conversation," he observed.

## 15

High fructose corn syrup
Tomato purée (water, tomato paste)
Vinegar
Molasses
Modified food starch
Apple cider vinegar
Salt
Honey
Natural smoke flavor
Mustard flour
Spice
Dried onions
Potassium sorbate (to preserve freshness)
Dried garlic

An excerpt from <u>www.dissingdoug.com</u>

*A Review of* Miss Wyoming

*Miss Wyoming* was one of Coupland's lesser-known books. It is about a pageant princess-cum-actress and a movie producer-turned burned-out drug addict-turned bohemian. The two protagonists are cosmically drawn together after taking a one-year hiatus from their oh-so-difficult lives of slightly dwindling fortune and fame. The story is told in an asynchronous fashion, jumping from past to present and back to past again.

Miss Wyoming isn't a bad read, necessarily, but there are a few problems with it. First, Coupland tries too hard to draw direct comparisons between the two protagonists' backgrounds. While the female "lead" had a life of pageantry thrust upon her, the male, in fact, pursued his own dreams and was crushed by them. Coupland considers a "Hollywood career" the most grinding of male pursuits. That is because Douglas Coupland lives, in essence, an insular life of well-funded artistic leisure. Sure, Hollywood is a grind compared to making LEGO statues for the municipal government of Vancouver for a million bucks a pop, but if you want to try a real grind that can fuck up a person's life, try writing about engineers for the oil industry, doctors, nurses, accountants, lawyers or the military. By choosing the characters he does, Coupland firmly cements his belief that the celebrity class sits head and shoulders above the rest of us meaningless peons. That's his right, to be sure, and it doesn't make for a bad book, but it does make the story somewhat unrelatable to anyone who doesn't have a trust fund or who has to work for a living. It's more like a twisted Disney fairy tale about a princess and a prince. Maybe that was his point. It's hard to tell, with artists.

My second issue with the book is the unidimensional exploration of pageant mothers. Basically, they're bad. They are the "evil witch" continuing the Disney analogy.  I would have liked the mother character to have a little more dimension. All people have a little bit of good or bad inside them. Explaining the mother's motivations might have been interesting. But, of course, politics come into play. Sympathizing with a pageant mother would be considered bad publicity, so instead of writing the hard thing, Coupland does the easy thing and cashes the ensuing cheques. Having thus ranted, I do suspect that a lot of us are in fact one-dimensional beings in a two-dimensional universe. (This reviewer is "the scatter-brained guy," to all who know him, as an example.)

What more can you expect from an "artist" who specializes in "design."

Having said all that, I still kind of liked this book. And who am I to tell someone what to write. To paraphrase Pontius Pilate, "What he has written, he has written."

I give it a B-minus. Fucking Coupland.

Well, we figured out what happened to Mahmoud and Frances – and now the proverbial shit is about to hit the proverbial fan. On a side note, there is no actual proverb in the Bible about shit and fans, so the analogy, I guess, is not technically "proverbial."

Ray pretty much nailed it, when it came to Frances. Some people just can't be helped, and can't be trusted. I can't believe I broke maki with him.  Still, I feel bad for him in a way. Maybe we didn't try hard enough to bring him into the fold. Maybe we let his peevishness, and bitterness drive a wedge between us. Sure we tried, but maybe we could have tried harder.

Part of me is annoyed that Frances figured out the Mahmoud secret before Clara and I could. It was supposed to be "our" secret, dammit. Maybe Frances will make for an OK reporter after all. He got his article published in the *National Post*.

Since then, Mom's apartment has been empty, and I've resumed my duty as koi-fish wrangler. I'm guessing he's long gone.

The following is his article:

## GRANTREPRENEURS:
### MAHMOUD'S STORY

*Mahmoud is a soft spoken, nervous man.* I met him while investigating one of Vancouver's new Super-Subsidized Startups, a grantrepreneurial hub known as A.I. Plus Womxn's Health Solutions.

Mahmoud, according to the company database, migrated to Canada from Syria, via a refugee camp in Turkey. His story is a compelling one. Having to leave his family behind in Turkey, he now works tirelessly to raise enough capital to sponsor their immigration. Or so the story goes.

Unlike so many newcomers, Mahmoud has managed a mastery of the English language, so dedicated is he to finding his loved ones and flying them here to join him in his new life as a Canadian success story.

Right away, after meeting Mahmoud, I knew something was off. I had learned Arabic in my former life as an economist who studied global oil supply, but when I greeted Mahmoud in what I thought surely must be his mother-tongue, he simply looked quietly in my direction without offering reply.

My next clue came at lunch. I followed him to La Taqueria Pinche. As he sat eating, I entered the establishment and sat across from him. Before him was a steaming plate of Tacos Al Pastor.

I confronted him. "It's chicken," he said, "I swear!"

But this reporter hadn't spent five years assessing agriculture and stockyard output to be fooled by the "other white meat."

"The jig is up," I told Mahmoud.

He took a deep breath and seemed almost relieved. Then he told me his story.

Mahmoud is not a Syrian immigrant. He is, in fact, an American heavy machinery operator named José Chavez from Los Angeles.

"I'd gone to Europe with a couple of friends after my divorce. We did a two-week singles bus tour to meet girls and have fun. It was great. My friends were from New York, and we hadn't seen one another for a long time.

"Just before we were supposed to come home, I got a call from work that I'd been laid off. I thought, 'what the heck,' and decided to change my plans. I booked a flight to Montreal to visit my sister who was working there at the time.

"The thing is though, because it was a last-minute booking, I had to fly from Paris to Istanbul, and then on to Montreal. I didn't mind. What was I rushing for? I didn't have a job to go back to.

"What happened is, when we got to Istanbul, everyone deplaned except me. The flight attendant checked and sure enough there's been some kind of error. The flight to Montreal was supposed to be a closed flight but somehow the empty seat had shown up and they'd been able to book it for me.

"Well, the plane loads up with these migrant families – like dozens of them. And these poor people are in pretty rough shape. I offered to give up my seat, realizing that this was one of the first immigration air flights to Canada, but there was nobody to take it so I kept it.

"Well, we arrived in Montreal, and there's this big crowd at the airport to welcome all the Syrians. And we're being paraded down this line, like it's a wedding reception or something, and I get close to the end of the line, and here's this guy, who looks awfully familiar, and he's putting winter coats on the Syrians and shaking their hands and welcoming them to Canada.

"Now, I'm not proud to say this, but it hadn't been that cold in Europe, and here I was in Montreal in the winter, and I only have a light fall jacket with me, and I see a guy giving out free coats. They had tons of them, and I figured there wouldn't be any harm, so I stayed in line and when I get to him, the prime minister shakes my hand, says 'Welcome home,' and puts this coat on me, you know, like Jesus washing his disciples' feet kind of thing, and without thinking, I say, 'Thanks, man.'

"Well, he gets this excited look on his face and starts talking 'English?' he says. 'You speak English?'

"'Yeah, sure,' I say, 'why?'

"'Oh man, I'm going to make you a superstar!' he says. All the while, the news cameras are flashing and there's a big ruckus, you know.

"I have this friend back in LA, we call him Mikey Chuckles. Mikey has this problem where he's always drinking NyQuil. He says it helps him mellow out. If I had to guess, I'd say the prime Minister was pretty 'Quilled up.'

"Anyway, he makes this big deal of taking me over to his

team and introducing me. I think one guy figured out the mistake. 'What's your name?' he asks. I tell him.

"He tries to confer with the prime minister, but the PM just waves him off. I heard him say 'Just figure it out,' and then he went back to the jackets.

"This guy lets out a big sigh. 'OK, José,' he says, 'a few things: Canada is your oyster. The boss is going to want to parade you around. You're going to make a shitload of money. Does that sound good to you?'

"'Sure,' I say. 'What's the catch?'

"'Your name. From now on, it's Mahmoud, OK? You do what you can to look and act like your real name is Mahmoud.'

"So we made a deal. I got a Canadian passport under the name Mahmoud El Habib. For about a year I was paraded around the country, being 'employed' by all these different businesses, always in the local media as an immigrant success story. It started getting me down. So I finally reached out to my handlers and begged them to park me somewhere, so I could gradually get back to my old life. They didn't know about L.A. per se. It was kind of 'don't ask don't tell,' kind of thing. But they knew it would be a big scandal if it ever got out what had happened.

"They said if I did one last job for them, they would move me anywhere I wanted to go. My sister had gone to Vancouver, so that's where I said.

"They set me up to do the grand opening of A.I. Plus Womxn's Health Solutions, and I've been here for about three months. The problem I have is that the company is still giving me paychecks, and there was a lot of news coverage of the grand opening because the PM was there. I was worried that if I just left, it would reflect poorly on the actual Syrian immigrants. Plus my job is pretty easy."

I asked José what his job is.

"I don't know. Something about a fishpond, I think. I also supply toilet paper to the men's washroom. Like I said, it's easy."

This reporter is left wondering what it will take for the average Canadian taxpayer to wake up to the grant and subsidy gong show that is driving us to borrow more than we can ever hope to repay.

*We were at the office* when the story broke. A phone rang at a desk at the bottom of the spiral marked "Reception." We had never heard it ring before. It kept ringing until Ray took it off the hook and unplugged it.

"What now?" I asked.

"I don't know," he said. "We need to find Ravi."

Mr. Singh's phone went straight to voicemail. Ray left a message. "Mr. Singh – there's an article that was just published in the National Post about Mahmoud and the company. Can you call us back and let us know what you'd like us to do?"

Within an hour, a small gathering had begun on the curb outside A.I. Plus Womxn's Health Solutions. Predominantly white-haired men in rumpled suits and sportscoats were shuffling about on the sidewalk. Some of them held signs that said "End Taxploitation," and "No Way, José!"

I heard crying coming from the women's room. I knocked and called in, "Clara? Are you OK?"

"This is my fault!" she said.

"No, honey, no," I said. "It's nobody's fault."

She came to the door and sniffed. "Did you just call me 'Honey?'"

I smiled. "I suppose I did."

"That's very sexist," she said. "I could file a complaint, you know."

"I'm sorry," I stammered. "I was just trying to, uh..."

"I'm in love with you," she said. She pulled me into the washroom and kissed me hard on the mouth. We made love, with her positioned on the "Easy-Kleen" Global Industries Baby Change Table. It had never been used before, so we figured it was sanitary.

One might argue that sex acts performed in a public restroom do not technically qualify as "Love making," but I speak from experience when I disagree with that sentiment.



It turns out that Frances had fallen pretty hard for Clara, and luckily for me, she'd already been in love with someone else. She told him as much, and he didn't take it well. Rejected and bitter, he had decided to go ahead with the story about Mahmoud.



We jostled our way through the crowd of grumpy protesters. "It's like night of the living unemployable out here," Ray said.

We walked home as a group instead of taking the Canada Line. The sun was brilliant and the day was hot, and I felt happy and loved despite the crumbling situation around us. Clara held my hand as we walked. I'm not usually much for human contact, but it felt wonderful.

"Try not to be too cheerful, you happy assholes," Ray said. "We still need to figure out a plan."

The four of us made a pact to stick together, regardless of what happened to A.I. Plus Womxn's Health Solutions. We were a team now.

My mom called to let us know that she and Wu were at the airport on their way home. I wanted to tell her about the National Post article, but Michael snatched the phone from me.

"Katherine," he said, "it's Michael. I hate to interrupt, but I really need to speak to Wu."

He waited a moment while she handed the phone over. "Wu," he said, "I'm in a bit of a pickle here. I ran out of medication while you were away. I got a prescription and started taking it, and, uh, well – I've been feeling pretty weird. Is there any way... oh... OK, just a sec."

Michael handed the phone to me. "He says he wants to talk to you."

"Hi, Wu," I said.

"Nicholas, Michael was never taking Ritalin. Those pills I give him are pure, uncut cocaine."

"I understand," I said.

"If you could let Lonnie know that Michael is out of medication, he will sort it out. There are prescription bottles with Michael's name on them in the house. I believe they are in the second-floor bathroom taped to the underside of the toilet-tank lid."

"Will do, Wu," I said.

"We'll be home in thirty-six hours. You and I are brothers now. I trust you to fix things for Michael. Michael is like another brother to me, and that means he is like a brother to you too."

"OK," I said.

"I love you, brother."

"Right back at you," I said, not really knowing what else to say. I had a new brother who ran an Asian drug cartel.

Wu hung up.

"Hmm," I said. "Wu says Lonnie has your pills."


Michael and I went to see Lonnie.

When we arrived, Wu's house was dark. The gate across the driveway was closed.

"I don't think he's here," I told Michael.

"Well doesn't that just take the cake," Michael said. "I really need my fix."

There was an intercom beside the gate and Michael pressed the buzzer, but there was no answer.

I tried to call Mom to find out if Lonnie had a cell phone we could try, but the call went straight to voicemail. We tried Wu next, but it was the same. They were obviously already in the air.

"Maybe we can sneak in around back," Michael said.

We crept through the trees that lined the fence. On the far side, we could hear the burbling water-feature. An old apple tree grew beside the high cedar wall.

"Do you think we can climb it?" Michael asked.

"How bad do you need your pills?" I asked.

"I don't want to overstate this," Michael said, "but I would happily eat a steaming pile of human excrement right now to get my hands on one."

"Let's hope it doesn't come to that," I said.

Michael shimmied easily up the tree and onto the parapet, then helped me so that we ended up straddling the wall over-looking the garden shed.

"Follow me," Michael said.

He placed one foot against the shed and one against the cedar wall and shimmied down between the two, like Ninja Spider-Man. He must have really been jonesing.

I tried to do the same, but as soon as I let my ankle take my weight, I fell in a heap on the grass. My body made a loud thump and I sucked wind, making a sound roughly as subtle as that made by an accelerating Boeing 747.

I lay there for a while, then got to my knees, and finally my feet. Nothing felt broken.

When I came around the edge of the garden shed, I was dismayed to find the decorative lighting had been turned on.

Lonnie sat next to the water feature. He was duct-taped to a patio chair, and had been taped so thoroughly that only his head and neck were visible above the silver cocoon.

Behind him, a man in brown Dockers with pale blue loafers, and a green, palm-frond-print Hawaiian shirt stood pointing a stylish, silenced, gold-and-enamel handgun at

Michael who was kneeling in the grass with his fingers inter-laced behind his head.

"Hi Nick," Frances said.

"Hi Frances," I said. "What's going on?"

"I saw you on the security monitor," Frances said, holding the tablet from Wu's kitchen to display an infrared live feed of the fence I'd just climbed. "That was quite a tumble."

"I'm not much of an athlete," I said. "How'd you guess the code?"

"These Chinese guys," he said. "They're crazy about their eights."

He stared at me a moment.

"I'm kind of new at this," he said, waving Wu's gold-plated handgun. "Do you think you could help me out?  I'd like to tape up Michael here.

"Don't help him," Lonnie said, "he's trying to screw Wu."

Nonchalantly, Frances pointed the gun at Lonnie and pulled the trigger. The gunshot sounded no louder than a sharp cough. The shot missed by a little over a meter and splashed into the koi pond. I heard a second splash almost immediately after and wondered if Wu had built a second pond further down. I remembered how bullets could ricochet off water.

"Whoa," I said, "take it easy Frances!  We aren't here to hurt you!"

"No? You aren't? Bull!" he shouted. "It's people like you who have completely destroyed my life!"

"Hey, we just met you," I said. "We gave you a job!"

"Yeah – sure you did. After you disassembled my entire existence piece by piece. First it was the taxes – the fucking taxes!  Forty-seven percent wasn't enough. It went to fifty. Then fifty-five. I lost my house!  I couldn't pay the goddamned mortgage!  All so fucking useless millennial grantrepreneurs like you shitheads can sit around a modern office building and Snapchat about how great liberalism is.

"Then came the identity politics!  It wasn't enough to have

an MBA from U of T. It wasn't enough to have a degree from the London School of Economics. Because I'm nothing but a Pale Stale Male, I lost my job altogether. The Fraser Institute – the one think tank meant to keep all this shit in check – can you guess who they hired to replace me? They hired a Chinese Transgendered Autistic Guy named David – aka Dolly – Chung. They used my position to fill all three of their diversity criteria. Does Dolly have a degree? No. Does Dolly know anything about economics? No. But what Dolly does have is hundred and fifty grand in government subsidy per year. So out with Frances, in with Dolly."

"I'm sorry, Frances," Michael said. "That blows. If you need money, you can have some of mine. But have you seen a brown prescription bottle with my name on it...."

"Oh shut up!" Frances said.

A plan began forming in my mind.

"So what does Wu have to do with all this?"

"I went through your company records. Did you know I could do that? Because you've applied for grant money through every branch of government, the Access to Information Act means I can find every single detail about A.I. Plus Womxn's Health Solutions. And guess who I found was co-founder of the company?"

"Michael J Fox?" Lonnie asked, helpfully.

"No," Frances yelled. "Not Michael J Fox. What the fuck? Wu Chung. Wu fucking Chung. David aka Dolly Chung's half-brother. It's fate that he should be tied up in all this. It's all so clear to me now. You assholes, Wu, David – it's like the cosmos have aligned and I can see my destiny. I have to kill Wu."

"Hmm… that clarity you're describing sounds like you might have found my pills," Michael said. "Can we do sharezees?"

"Wu is on a plane from Hong Kong," I said. He should be here within the next twenty-four hours though."

"Fine," Frances said. "We'll wait."

Frances pointed the pistol at me while I taped up Michael, then he taped me to an Adirondack chair beside Lonnie.

He then started storming back and forth across the lawn, muttering to himself. I remembered how Clara had handled him when we'd first met him.

"Uh, Frances," I said. "Remember the koi pond at the office?"

"What?" He snapped back to reality for a moment. "Yes, sure."

"That water feature over there is actually another koi pond," I said. "It's why we're here. We're supposed to feed them."

"So what?" he said.

"Well, the thing is, I mean you might hate our guts and everything, but you really shouldn't take it out on the fish. You seemed to really enjoy them back at the office."

"Yes – they're very elegant," he said.

"Since we're tied up, would you mind feeding them?" I asked.

"Seriously?"

"Yeah," I said. "I don't want the koi to starve."

"Fuck," he said. "OK. Where's the food?"

"It's over by the shed, in that big bucket," Lonnie said. "They only take one scoop."

"Fine," Frances growled.

He stooped down and scooped a handful of koi food, and walked back to the pond. He stared at the water for a moment.

"You know," he said, "I can't quite explain it but I find the site of the koi fish incredibly pacifying."

He tossed in the pellets, and the surface roiled. I tensed myself to charge him, hoping I could move the Adirondack enough to push him into the pond. But just as I was about to try, a seventeen-inch silver carp exploded like a rocket from the water feature, arcing through the air, and hitting Frances, who was dressed, as I would later realize, just like a decorative potted palm, square in the gonads.

"Ooof," he said, doubling over.

There was a barking cough sound, and a red mist erupted from the back of Frances' head.  His body tumbled forward into the water.

"Oh shit," I said. I tried to move but I was stuck. The Adirondack wouldn't even budge.

Lonnie craned his neck to see. "I think he just shot himself in the head."

"Hmm," said Michael, "Lonnie, do you know where Wu keeps my Ritalin?"


We spent the entire night sitting there, duct-taped to Wu's lawn furniture. My cell phone rang a few times, but I was unable to reach into my pocket to get it.

"Why did you tape me up so tight?" Michael asked.

"I didn't want him to shoot me," I said. "Sorry man."

"How come you told him to feed the fish?  What were you hoping to accomplish?"

"I didn't realize how stuck I am," I explained. "I was going to push him into the pond so he would drop his gun."

"Smart," Lonnie said. "By the way, do either of you guys happen to have any heroin on you?  I could really use a little vein candy."

"How about my Ritalin, Lonnie?" Michael asked. "I'm in need too."

"It isn't Ritalin," I said. "It's cocaine."

"Well, that certainly explains some things," Michael said.

"In a way, it's better," said Lonnie. "You can get cocaine just about anywhere. Ritalin, you either need a script or you have to steal it from kids."

They got into a discussion about the economics of the illicit drug trade relative to the pharmaceutical industry while I sat and watched the lights over English Bay, and listened to the fish eat Frances. Eventually Lonnie had a withdrawal seizure and Michael fell asleep.

Ray arrived around ten o'clock the next morning. We didn't know it was Ray, of course, but we could hear the intercom buzzing. Not wanting to call out, in case it was the police, we waited. Finally, we heard rustling from the apple tree. A second later there was a thump and the jet-engine sound of someone trying to get their wind.

Since we'd been found at that point, I called over, "Are you OK?"

"No," wheezed Ray. "I can't breathe."

"Ray?" Michael said.

He emerged, limping, from behind the shed and examined the scene. Three grown men were duct-taped to lawn furniture. A fourth man floated dead in the koi pond. He didn't ask any questions. He just produced his pocketknife and began cutting through the tape.

"I thought we'd lost you guys," he said, hugging each of us as we were freed. "I thought you ran."

"We just came for my Ritalin," Michael said. "It turns out it's cocaine."

Ray examined the body in the koi pond. "Did you murder Frances?" he asked, looking. at me.

"Do you think I'm capable of murder?" I said.

"Anyone can be capable of it," he said.

"Then why didn't you look at Lonnie and Michael when you asked?"

"Oh. They aren't capable of it."

He had a point. "Truth be told, the fish did it," I said, pointing at the silver carp desiccating on the grass. Ray hiked an eyebrow. "He's dressed like a potted palm."

"Ah," Ray said. "And the missing piece of his head with the koi fish in it?"

I looked. Sure enough, a brilliant white and orange metallic Hariwake koi swam gracefully between the waving fibrous tissue strands that rippled in and out of the gaping exit wound.

"He wasn't so up to date on firearm safety."

"Gotcha," Ray said. "So, like…" He pantomimed a fish hitting him in the crotch, then grabbed at his groin, doubled over and accidentally shot himself in the head. When he did the head shot part, he waggled his fingers to simulate the brain matter flying out.

"Exactly," Michael said. "Can we please go inside for my coke now?"


I saw that Clara had called twice through the night. I was quite touched. I made to call her back, and Ray stopped me.

"She's pretty upset," he said. "There's something you should see."

He opened his phone to the CTV news app. The first news story was titled "Subsidies and Exploitation in Vancouver Business"

He clicked on the video, and we watched an ad for the new Kia Sorento as it loaded. "They aren't bad," Michael said. "My mom drives one."

After the ad, the footage was of a media scrum huddled around a tanning salon on Davie Street. Mr. Singh emerged from the salon, and nearly jumped when he saw the gathering of cameras and reporters.

They jostled to get close to him, shouting unintelligible questions.

"A tanning salon?" Michael asked.

"Just watch," Ray said.

The CTV news reporter was shoved roughly from behind, and fell into Singh. It gave her a chance to ask him a question.

"Mr. Singh, is it true that you aren't really Sikh?"

"Ahh…"

"Are you really Mike McAllister from Fort McMurray?"

"No comment," Singh said.

The footage jumped back to the anchorwoman in studio.

"As many of you know, an employee list for the Vancouver startup A.I. Plus Womxn's Health Solutions became public today, and details are still emerging of what some are describing as the largest grant and subsidy scam in Canadian history.

"Among the subsidies being exploited by the company? Immigration employment grants and green building grants, as well as employment subsidies for the disabled, for the recently incarcerated, for gender fluidity, the mentally ill, and the sex worker safety initiative.

"Absent from the list of employees is CEO Ravi Singh, a Sikh Vancouverite who has rapidly climbed the ranks of the province's wealthiest citizens.

"In this photo, you can see an image of Mr. Singh alongside a picture of Michael McAllister, formerly of Fort McMurray, who has been missing since the Alberta wildfire of 2016."

McAllister looked exactly like Singh, only without the turban and with lighter skin.

"It was learned that a person using Mr. McAllister's credit card has been booking bi-weekly tanning sessions at Slippery Chip's Tanning Salon in West Vancouver.

"When confronted about the fraud allegations, Mr. Singh offered no comment.

"This morning in parliament, the leader of the official opposition had this to say:"

The footage jumped to the steps of parliament, where an angry, flushed man breathlessly addressed an assembled crowd.

"Today we learned that there might be an exploitation scandal involving a company intimately associated with the prime minister. I will be personally flying to Vancouver within the next seventy-two hours to assess the situation on the ground. I hope the RCMP will do their due diligence in determining if a crime has been committed. Canadian taxpayers deserve better. Thank you."

Ray turned off the phone.

"Well?" I asked.

"There's something else," he said.

He opened another webpage. It was a list of employees and grants/subsidies associated with them.

He scrolled down the list of names and then stopped. He pointed to one name in particular. I read it, and felt the blood drain from my face.

"Sex worker?"

He opened another tab on his phone. It was a webpage with a blown-up photo of Clara. She wore a latex body suit and held a riding crop in her teeth. The banner across the top read, "Ms. Clara – Concubine to the Stars."

I couldn't speak.

"What should we do?" asked Michael.

"Nick needs to go talk to Clara. You and Lonnie and I are going to fish Frances out of the koi pond." He checked his watch. "Hopefully Wu will know what to do with the body."

"What about A.I. Plus Womxn's Health Solutions?" Lonnie asked.

"I have an idea," Ray said, "but it's going to take a lot of work."

"How much work?" Michael asked, "I'm hungry and I need drugs."


Clara wasn't in the apartment. Her stuff was gone from her bedroom. I tried the apartment upstairs, the one I still wasn't allowed to see (and now I thought I knew why) but she didn't answer. Not knowing what else to do, I left the building and walked down to the dog park, feeling more alone than I'd ever felt before.

I sat on the bench, the one I'd thought of as "our bench," and tried not to cry. I tried not to cry for all the things that could have been, and for my dad, and for my messed-up family and even for Frances, who hadn't been such a bad guy, who had just failed to transition from an older time.

After a while, the feeing went away, and I watched the pretty women in yoga pants and their dogs, and I wondered if dogs were capable of comprehending loss.

Clara sat down beside me. "What are you thinking about?" she asked.

"I was just wondering about how, you know, when a dog owner dies, and the dog is stuck in the house with the dead owner, and eventually they eat the owner – I was wondering if the dog feels guilt. Since they never eat the owner right off, they wait until they're pretty hungry, I'd have to guess that they do feel guilt. But having said that, does the fact that they eventually eat the body mean that a dog inherently believes in the presence of a soul?"

She shivered. "That head of yours."

We sat for a minute and then she turned to me. Huge tears were threatening to spill down her cheeks. "It wasn't sex," she started. "I'm more like, a psychologist to these people. I mean…"

I cut her off. "Clara, I don't care," I said. "I love you either way."

Tears spilled down her face and she hugged me tight. I could smell lavender and fall leaves in her hair and on her neck. "I love you," she said.

We held one another like that for what felt like hours, and only broke our embrace when a springer spaniel squatted for a shit six inches from my left shoe.

"I'm so sorry," the yoga-panted dog owner said, as she stooped with a plastic bag to clean up the dog's leavings.

Laughing, I told her it was fine.

"So what do we do now?" Clara asked.

"Apparently Ray has some kind of plan."

We walked back to the apartment hand in hand. Nobody

was home. We made love twice. I was falling asleep when she ripped a piece of duct tape off my neck.

"Yowch!" I yelled.

"What's with the duct tape?"

"Frances took us hostage while he was waiting to ambush Wu," I explained, "but he was hit with a carp that mistook him for a potted palm and accidentally shot himself in the head."

"Oh," she said.

We slept in each other's arms.

I awoke to my cell phone ringing. It was Dr. Chu's resident, Emily. "We need to meet," she said.


The sun was going down when Clara and I reached the Vancouver General Hospital. We met Emily in the pathology lab. She was working with another young woman whom I assumed to be the pathology resident.

"OK, we're here," I said. "What's up?"

"It's the koi serum," Emily said.

"What about it?"

"We tested it for regrowth of lobules, and it doesn't work."

"Well, that sucks," I said.

"But I still had some serum leftover so I did some other tests. Call it scientific curiosity. I called Deb here, who does most of our cancer research, and she let me use some of her adenocarcinoma clones. The koi serum appears to be oncostatic. It suppressed mitosis amongst cell lines that express the oncogene for DCIS."

"It's very exciting," Deb said.

"I'm not sure I understand," Clara said.

"Do you have a science background?" Emily asked.

"I'm a classically trained dominatrix."

"Oh," said Deb. "Well, to put it simply, DCIS is an early form of cancer and koi serum seems to stop it from growing."

"If they can figure out how to administer it, they'll probably want to use it for every patient who gets diagnosed and then has to wait for surgery. It could prevent the cancer from growing."

"And that's just the DCIS," Emily said. "We haven't even begun to look at other malignancies."

"So… we found a treatment for breast cancer?" Clara said.

"Essentially, yes, we've discovered a new weapon for the arsenal."

"And it comes from koi fish."

"Uh huh."

"We need to make some phone calls."

# 16

Barley malt vinegar
Spirit vinegar
Molasses
Sugar
Salt
Anchovies
Tamarind extract
Onions
Garlic
Spice
Flavorings


An excerpt from www.dissingdoug.com

*A Review of Monument to the War of 1812 (Toy Soldiers)*

Toy Soldiers is a Coupland sculpture in Toronto. I have to admit, I like this one. At first glance, from a distance, you think it's a standard bronze war memorial, but on closer inspection, you see that there is a bronze British toy soldier, complete with rough molding seam, standing over a toppled, silver, American toy soldier. The footpads immediately throw you back to your childhood days of playing with "Army guys."

The piece is significant for a few reasons. To a pacifist, it resonates, without being disrespectful to the men who fought. I inherently dislike the way our soldiers are treated like nothing more than toys by politicians, their lives no more valuable than plastic scrap. Secondly the British resistance of the Americans is a big part of Canadian history, and third, this installment, though classic Coupland tongue-in-cheek kitsch, looks like it would have been quite difficult and time consuming to create. I was not surprised then, to learn it had been privately commissioned.


Ravi Singh (aka Mike McAllister) was in the wind. Clara, Jeff, Michael's Cocaine (now happily balanced and fortified by his small daily-dose regimen), Lonnie and I worked through the first night, locating everyone on the employee list of A.I. Plus Womxn's Health Solutions and calling them back to work. Singh had been smart about one thing, he'd kept everyone on the payroll, skimming only a percentage for the company. When we explained that the business was in trouble, they agreed to come in without hesitation.

We broke down the list by type of subsidy we were receiving. I went over PQRS – which meant "Physically Disabled," "Queer and gender fluid," "Recovering from abusive relationship," "Refugee status," and "Syrian."

About halfway through my list, I turned to Ray. "I don't like the way we're pigeonholed into these categories. I spoke to two gender-fluid employees in a row, and they're totally different people, and yet according to this, they are considered just this one thing."

"Dude," he said, "it's identity politics. It's so politicians can tell big swaths of society how to vote. That's it. We know it's bullshit. But that bullshit is our gravy train. So hold your fucking nose if you have to, and keep making calls."

He patted me on the back.

"Yes sir," I said. "But I have to say, if my one-dimensional life were building to some kind of moral theme, I'd say, if anything, our unsubtle dialogue just now was a bit 'in your face,' you know?"

"Sometimes you just have to come right out and say it. People are idiots. You kind of have to spoon-feed them. Anyway, it's not like your life is up for a Giller Prize. Why be subtle?"

In that, he had an excellent point.

I had trouble with the Arabic-speaking refugees. I got as far as "Mar-Haban, ana ismee Nick" which I'm hoping means "hello, my name is Nick," but I had yet to learn any Arabic and most of them had yet to learn much English. I asked Michael's Cocaine for help.

"Oh, actually, there's this one guy named Syed who's in my English as a Second Language course. Let's see..." he scrolled through my list. "Hey this might be him," he said.

He called Syed, who it turns out, could speak fluent English after only two months of classes. I made a mental note to register for an ESL course. Syed was in an apartment with three other Syrian workers and recruited them to come in. "We'd been waiting for the building to be ready," he told Michael's Cocaine.

"Oh, as it turns out, we were initially just some kind of employment scam, but now we have actual work to do in order to avoid having the company shut down. Actually, on a personal note, we're likely all at risk of going to prison if we don't pull this off."

"I understand," Syed said. We gave him the address, and he and his co-habitants came to the apartment and took over the Arabic-Speaking employee calls.

Mom and Wu Chung knocked on the door.

"Who is the dead man in my garden shed?" Wu asked.

"Frances McCain," I said.

"Poor Frances," Wu said. "I was worried that the anger he carried might be too much for him. How did he get my gun?"

"He guessed your code. 8888. You should think about changing it."

"Oh, no, I could not," Wu said. "It is lucky."

"Is it?" I asked. "It wasn't for Frances."

"It was for me," he said. He had a point.

After a moment, I said, "Did you know your brother, David, now Dolly, replaced Frances at the Fraser Institute?"

"Yes. That was done purposefully after Frances wrote a piece about Chinese gangs influencing the longshoremen and disrupting intercontinental trade."

"I see," I said.

"I have people everywhere. It's kind of how being the head of an international crime syndicate works."

I explained everything that was happening with A.I. Plus Womxn's Health Solutions. Wu smiled when I finished.

"So they finally found out about Mike?" he said. "That's funny. I have to see this video. I bet it's hilarious."

"You knew?"

"Of course," Wu said. "Mike McAllister used to work for me in Fort McMurray. He owed me quite a bit of money, and after the fire, we devised a way for him to pay it back. By assuming the identity of Ravi Singh, he was able to infiltrate the insular Sikh business community."

"He sold drugs to the Sikhs?"

"No, he sold Kias to them. We opened a dealership together."

"Michael *is* quite fond of the Sorento," I said.

"I've had many vehicles," Wu said, "But I regard none as fondly as my Sorento. It did everything I asked of it and more."

Mom wanted to tell us all about Tokyo and Hong Kong, but because we were so pressed for time, we had to send her in search of lab coats and safety glasses. "We need about two hundred," I said, handing her the A.I. Plus Womxn's Health Solutions credit card.

Ray went to see Coupland.


Late in the afternoon, Lonnie, who had lost all the hair from the back of his head during the duct-tape ordeal, said he needed to "inject some happiness" into his afternoon, and took off for Wu's house.

Mom called and told us she found tons of lab coats at a

Halloween party supply store, but she needed help getting them back. Jeff left to help.

Michael's Cocaine left at five o'clock to catch his English as a Second Language course, and Syed and his roommates all left at the same time. "I can't miss tonight, guys," Michael's Cocaine said. "We're covering Alexandrine French Heroic verse. It's supposed to be a game changer."

Clara and I were alone in the apartment when her phone rang. She looked at the screen. It showed a picture of a well-known retired CTV News anchor. The man had to be in his eighties. "Uh oh," she said, angling the screen so I could see better. "He's kind of fucked up."

"You can get it," I said.

"Naw," she said. "I think I'm done with the dominatrix stuff." She declined the call.

"How is he fucked up?" I asked.

"Well, he's quite old you know. Do you remember the way he looked on TV, with the pancake makeup? Remember how they always gave him those flushed looking cherubic cheeks? Well, he's convinced that it's funeral-home makeup and that he's died and been reanimated. He might be suffering the early stages of Lewy Body Dimentia, now that I think about it."

"Right. What do you do for him?"

"Do you really want to know?"

"Sure."

"I get dressed in this early-nineteenth-century outfit, with the blouse and corset and whatnot. He puts on his suit, and does his makeup, and then he does my makeup, and then we go down to his basement where he has these two coffins beside one another. And we get in them and he cries for a while. He says his fantasy is to be buried beside somebody. He doesn't want to be in the ground all alone."

"That's, like, really sad."

"Yeah. But then, when he thinks I've fallen asleep, he jerks off in his coffin."

"Oh," I said.

"Yeah."

We were through with the phone calls. "Why don't I show you my place upstairs?" she said.

I don't know what I was expecting. Red lights and leather whips and ball-gags, I suppose, but the apartment looked more like an IKEA catalogue. Tasteful taupe furniture was complimented by soft lamps and colorful accent pillows. A sewing machine sat by the window.

"You sew?"

"When I have downtime."

"Do you, uh, entertain clients up here?"

"Oh no," she said. "Out calls only. You saw how weird it was with the prime minister."

"He's a client?"

"Yeah – I mean, he was. Like I said though, Ms. Clara is no more."

"What was he like?"

She thought about it. "Take the most fucked-up childhood celebrity you can imagine and crossbreed them with Paris Hilton and Osama Bin Laden, add a Nelson Mandela fascination, a Christ complex, and a psychotic mother and subsequent mommy issues. Throw in a tiny measure of Pol Pot and Charlie Manson and you're about a third of the way there. The cough syrup kind of keeps it under control."

"So why the apartment?"

"I don't like sharing a bathroom. Especially with a bunch of guys. Yick."

I walked around the flat, marveling at the normality of it. When I came to the bedroom I stopped. The closet was open, and inside I could see, among the jeans and sweaters and plaid shirts, a leather corset.

She saw me looking. "Oh, this? Like me to try it on?"

"No," I said. "I've never really been into that stuff."

"You know," she said, "I've been working on something that might be more your style."

She shooed me out of the room and I sat on the couch while she talked through the door. "I kind of had this idea, after that first day we went to the park together. I went to Fabricville and well, voila!"

She opened the door. It took me a second to figure out what was happening. Clara wore pajamas that appeared to be made from a dozen dogs.

"Remember that Simpson's episode, where Mr. Burns kills animals to make his clothing?" She began singing "... see my sweater, nothing better, than authentic Irish Setter."

"Uh huh," I said.

"Well it gave me the idea – I mean this is all synthetic, you know, but you get the idea."

She came to the couch and lay down with her head in my lap. "Pet me," she said.

"Isn't that degrading?"

"Degrading?"

"If I pet you like a dog?"

"Is it degrading for me to want you to feel at peace?"

"No."

"So, pet me, Nick. I like being petted."

I petted her. After a while my mind went completely tranquil and I very nearly fell asleep.

She sat up and whispered in my ear. "You like it, don't you?"

"It's nice," I said.

"See," she said, "we're all weirdos."

She stripped out of the furry pajamas, and led me to the bedroom.

# 17

Corn starch
Salt
Wheat flour
Modified corn starch
Glucose solids
Dextrose
Hydrolyzed soy and corn protein
Onion powder
Canola oil
Caramel color (sulfites)
Spices
Monosodium glutamate
Torula yeast
Xanthan gum
Tomato powder
Citric acid
Soy flour
Garlic powder
Beet powder
Herbs
Natural and artificial flavors
Disodium inosinate
Guanylate

An excerpt from www.dissingdoug.com

*A Review of* Microserfs *by Douglas Coupland*

*Microserfs* is sacrosanct. It cannot be skewered. *Microserfs* is the only novel to capture that period of hope in the mid 1990's when technology could solve things without fucking up the world.  People were making money. America's brain trust owned the known universe.

Weirdly, and this isn't really a criticism of the book, the first half of the story takes place in Redmond. It was published in 1995. Although none of the characters are particularly interested in music, I would have thought that Kurt Cobain's suicide the previous year would have warranted a line of dialogue. Having said that, maybe it sat between the word processor and the editor's desk for a year or two.

I can't criticize this book. It is far and away better than anything I'll ever write.

So here, instead, are some random personal thoughts I've had when reading it:

— Being a geek in the 90's was fun. My best friend and I were into computers. I ended up in science and then medicine, but always secretly wished I could work at Microsoft. Even now, after Apple and Google have made Silicon Valley the place for the cool kids, I'd rather work at Microsoft, where a quiet, benevolent genius founded an enormous team of hard-working gifted geeks who completely changed the world. My friend who went into engineering ended up at an IT campus in New Brunswick. They do something with switchgear and have changed ownership six times. Neither of us made it more than six months before losing the dream. The dream doesn't exist anymore. Succeed and everyone hates you. Fail and you can't pay your mortgage. But the dream used to exist. *Microserfs* reminds us of what that was like.

— I miss the times when technology helped us but didn't try to replace us.

— It's nice to be reminded of what it was like to be excited about things.


The big inspection day arrived and we really weren't sure how it would play out. Clara and I had overslept (of all days, for God's sake). We woke in a panic and hustled to catch the Sky Train, and just like our first day at A.I. Plus Womxn's Health

Solutions, we arrived to a sizable media scrum surrounding a makeshift stage and podium outside the building. Along with the news vans and reporters, I couldn't help but notice a contingent of VPD and RCMP. The leader of the opposition, whose name nobody can ever remember, stood, arms folded, at the edge of the crowd.

To my surprise, Coupland was at the microphone. Standing next to him was a small, curly-haired woman who looked vaguely familiar. Ray and Mr. Singh were on the stage by the corner steps. When Ray noticed us, he gave a subtle wink. A banner ran across the background. It bore a repeating pattern of thousands of tiny LEGO figures of all different ethnicities. Scrolled across the top, in LEGO, of course, was the caption "Diversity in the Digital Age." Classic Coupland.

A public address system carried his voice.

"... and no installation to date has required this extent of planning, funding or good old-fashioned elbow grease. Ms. Atwood and I cannot take full credit for this piece. That would be much the same as parents taking credit for the accomplishments of their adult child. But we did conceive this project together and have, fascinated, watched it grow organically.

"I'll move aside now so Margaret can explain the concept, and what you'll see inside today."

The small woman stepped to the podium. There were polite chuckles while she adjusted the microphone cluster, accentuating the size differences between herself and Doug.

"A.I. Plus Womxn's Health Solutions was designed to cut through platitudes and showcase the real power of combining biotechnology, art, workforce diversity, tolerance and feminism. Mr. Coupland and I believe that when too much is made of history, the present is prevented from turning into the future. We devised a way of artificially injecting a sense of the present into the workplace. McAllister 2.0 is a work by Douglas Coupland and I. It represents the first time that a living person and his ongoing biography have been used as a medium in a piece of artwork. After Mike McAllister lost his home in the Alberta Wildfire in 2016, I happened to sit next to him on a fateful flight from Edmonton to Toronto. Mike expressed to me his desire to erase everything he knew about himself, and to rise from the ashes of his former life, a completely new person. I set a meeting with Mike and Doug for the following morning, since Douglas and I had been discussing just such a project as McAllister 2.0 for years.

"We sent a sample of Mike's DNA to a genetic ancestry service, and asked him to pick one culture from his genetic ancestry to adapt. He was genetically 3.125% East Indian, so he decided to start living life as an Indian man. After researching Indian culture, he was able to choose Sikhism as his religious background.

"Ravi Singh is McAllister 2.0. He is a practicing Sikh. He has become a pivotal member of the Sikh business community and he identifies 100% as an Indian businessman. Sure, there will be much pearl-clutching and gnashing of teeth at the concept, but like any powerful art project, it is our hope that McAllister 2.0 will create discussion that leads to progress. In this case, much like gender fluidity, we hope to spark a new wave of recognition for the culturally and racially fluid.

"When we began the behemoth undertaking that is A.I. Plus Womxn's Health Solutions, we knew that installing McAllister 2.0 as the Chief Executive was not just the perfect fit, but also, given his ambition, strength of character and business savvy, the best hope we had of succeeding. We planted the seed with Mr. Singh – a research and development biotechnology company with a diverse workforce, housed in a building that is an essentially monument to progress, with the lofty goal of making strong, rapid advances in women's health research.

"A.I. Plus Womxn's Health Solutions' key researcher, Dr. Jennifer Chu, is with us this morning and will explain our first major breakthrough. A copy of her white paper, which is the featured article in *volume 1 issue 1* of our *Women's Health*

*Solutions Journal*, I should add, is being circulated to you currently."

Something bumped my leg and I peered down. A man who at first appeared to be just a torso and head had bumped me with his motorized wheelchair. I saw that he had small, disfigured hands, one of which controlled the mechanism, the other of which clutched a sheaf of papers. "Take one and pass them along, please," he said in a smokey, cafeteria-worker voice.

I did as he asked.

The paper was titled "*Cyprinus carpio* Serum as an Oncostatic Chemotherapy Agent in Ductal Carcinoma in Situ: an In vitro Analysis."

Dr. Chu took the microphone. "We've basically found a new treatment for breast cancer," she said. The crowd actually applauded.

"By analyzing the effect of serum from the koi fish used in the indoor invasive species farm, we were able to determine that the serum itself can prevent cell division in pre-invasive ductal cancer cells. These are the cells that cause the calcifications that radiologists like me search for on your mammogram.

"The next phase of study will be the administration of serum to patients waiting for surgery, to assess safety and efficacy. We are hoping to expedite ethics approval, given the strong *in vitro* results we've established. I'm happy to announce that the project has been awarded a Canadian Research Grant for two million dollars."

Applause sounded again. I checked, and sure enough, the leader of the opposition was smiling and clapping along with everyone else.

Next, there was a tour of the spiraling office space following the media scrum. The place was bustling.

Everyone wore lab coats. People in wheelchairs zipped from cubicle to cubicle. Syrians in safety glasses smiled and chatted in Arabic amongst themselves beside the koi pond. One woman wore a lab coat over her burka. I wondered if it might not be a bit "too much."

Computer screens were left on, strategically showing pages of a scientific nature. In the lab, the centrifuge spun endlessly as the elderly Chinese woman I'd stood next to on opening day sat beside it, supervising.

Clara and I followed the tour up the spiral. At one point, I saw the leader of the opposition hanging back. He approached us. "Ms. Clara," he said, "are you a part of all this?"

"Yes," she said.

"Do you still make appointments?"

She smiled sweetly. "No, hon, I'm afraid I don't. The R&D here takes up so much of my time."

He studied her, clearly wondering if this was some kind of blackmail ploy. "Is all this stuff for real?" he asked.

"As far as I know," she said. "I'm more on the Fisheries and Oceans side."

"You aren't going to, uh..."

She put a hand on his shoulder and pecked him on the cheek. "Your secret's safe with me."

He thanked her and walked away.

I whispered in her ear. "What kind of freaky stuff is the leader of the opposition into?"

"You know," she said, "it's funny. I don't remember him at all."


After the tour, the media gathered on the sidewalk outside. At Ray's cue, all the employees lined up in front of the building, with Ravi Singh standing front and center, smiling and proudly wearing his turban. Cultural appropriation or progress? Dammit, it wasn't entirely clear. Politics had been masterfully used against itself. I felt... very proud to be friends with Ray.

"Are you still planning an investigation?" someone from the media shouted to the leader of the opposition.

He fidgeted for a moment, and turned to see our workforce

– a crowd of faces, black, yellow, white and brown, men, women, trans, gay, straight, bi, able-bodied, disabled, young and old, and you could see the calculations of voter isolation running through his brain. He glanced at Clara and held her gaze for a full five seconds. Finally, he spoke.

"Sometimes, in politics, we get things wrong," he began.

# 18

*Ray took us all sneaker shopping.* We had each made more money in three months than I had expected to accumulate in twenty years of work as a medical specialist. My loans were paid off, and for the first time in my life, I had money in a savings account. Still, Ray insisted on paying for our sneakers. "You guys are my friends," he said. "Consider it symbolic."

He bought me a pair of Air Jordans, which I decided to wear proudly. Every time I go for a coffee, people will assume I'm a leisure class writer.

The day of the A.I. Plus Womxn's Health Solutions story, the prime minister suffered an "accidental overdose," of dextromethorphan in a hotel suite at the Royal York in Toronto. According to the media, he'd been suffering from severe sinusitis and had accidentally taken too frequent a dose. His wife and his chief of staff were said to be rushing back from a trade mission in Tahiti to be by his side while he recovered. Our story was all but buried.

We met with Douglas Coupland, who was extremely bitter about having to share credit for A.I. Plus Womxn's Health Solutions and McAllister 2.0 with Ms. Atwood.

"If you think my work is heavily subsidized, you should have a look at hers!" he complained. "She's like a relentless goddamned vacuum hose, sucking up every scrap of grant money from coast to coast."

"It was the only way to make it believable," Ray said. "Besides, we really had to bribe your ass to convince you to take the risk in the first place. You're making out pretty sweet in all this."

"It isn't about how much I make," he explained, "it's about how much other artists can't get. It isn't easy being king, you know."

"All that said," Ray smiled, "you did make a shitload."

"I underestimated how well you could pull it off," Coupland admitted. "I mean, McAllister 2.0 – it's so – unlikely."

"Wait! McAllister 2.0 wasn't real?"

Everyone looked at me like I had drool dripping off my chin.

"Unbelievable," I said.


Wu bought a house for Mom. He said he found the concept of his mother living in an apartment "distressing." She has convinced him to get out of the drug business, and they go to church together every Sunday. Jeff and I are a little bit jealous.

"You know," Wu told me, "the drug business was very cut-throat. I've found working with you folks nearly as lucrative and a lot less stressful. If the fish business works out, I'm going to have more money than most small European nations. I think it's all for the best, really."

While they were in Tokyo, Wu had purchased five thousand show-quality koi. He then shipped them to Hong Kong where a lab team worked on selective genetic breeding to build a single super-species of robust, highly fertile pond-fish.

He commissioned a shipbuilding conglomerate to convert an oil tanker to a live-tank, and to build a surface skimming live-trap tugboat for recapturing the fish. He and Doug incorporated a new business as Chungland Fishery Solutions.

The tanker is set to arrive in Vancouver next week.


Not since the Olympics has an event in Vancouver been so heavily promoted. Coupland's "Jewel of the Northwest," is being heralded as a landmark meeting of art, biology and environmental science." Hotels in Vancouver are booked solid for the event.

Michael's book, "Condimenting," was picked up by Harper Collins. It hasn't been officially announced yet, but there's a lot of speculation that it will be the first recipe-slash-self-help title to be nominated for a Giller Prize or PEN Award. Ray is filling out a nomination to have Michael named next years' National Poet Laureate.

Clara and I have moved into her place. I miss living with the guys, but her bed is a lot more comfortable than the couch. She still prefers me to use the other washroom though. We are looking at getting a dog.

Jeff is replacing the butcher paper in his window with stained glass. He found an artist at the Granville Island Market who will build it to his specifications. He chose an image of a fat, naked old man holding an umbrella. "It really symbolizes the Vancouver experience," he said.

Ray opened an indoor rock pigeon farm in Richmond. The preserve, called "The Center for the Study of Domestic Urban Wildlife," was featured as an eco-friendly example of entrepreneurship deserving of subsidy in the most recent federal budget. A.I. Plus Womxn's Health Solutions is formulating a buyout offer as early research indicates that *Columbia livia* egg albumen may have a role in the treatment of endometriosis.

Since Wu is getting out of the drug business, Michael has had to part ways with his cocaine addiction. The first few days were pretty rough, but he seems to have managed an otherwise smooth migration into caffeine and Wellbutrin. "It's like living a happy nightmare," he told me. I'm not sure what he means.

Lonnie is officially working as the Chungland Fishery Solutions accountant. He stated that he is trying to ween off smack to the full extent possible whereby he can still claim Wu's property as a safe injection site.

## 19

Burnout
Heartache
Fear
Depression
Anxiety
Monosodium glutamate
Grief
Numbness
Change
Asperger's
Friendship
Experience
Time off
Fun
Art
Celebrities (Canadian content)
*Canus Domesticus*
*Cyprinus Carpio*
*Cyprinus Carpio* extract
Love
Sex
Weird sex
Dominance
Mountains
Family
Chinese gangs
Condiments
Potassium sorbate (as preservative)
Joy
Natural flavors

*Clara and I held hands* standing behind the potted palms that lined the entire civilian walkway and bike path that ran the length of False Creek. Jeff, Mom, Michael, Michael's Tinder date, Vanessa, Mr. Singh and Ray stood with us.

"You know," Clara said, "this has been a really interesting few months."

Jeff, a little tipsy from cooking sherry, put his arms over our shoulders and pulled us together. "Can you guys believe it?" he asked for the fiftieth time. "I can't believe it."

"We know," I said.

A couple of days ago, he, Michael, and Ray sold Umbreller to the federal government. It sold for a staggering sum, and now my brother is a wealthy man.

"We're happy for you guys," I said. "Really."

"You assholes are so in love," he said. "You're glowing."

"It's true," Clara said. "We've grown very fond of one another."

As the sun set, Coupland's holograms came to life. Giant holographic LEGO koi fish were projected at intervals, hovering over the water, suspended over the rooftops of the buildings around us, and even on the distant mountains. It was an impressive effect. The fact that he was able to build it for one third the cost of the Arts Council budget by having the projectors mass produced in Hong Kong was not lost on me. Still, it was breathtaking. A roaring cheer erupted from the city.

Coupland stood on a barge at the mouth of the harbor, and a pillar of light shot skyward from the vessel. That was our cue to open the YouTube livestream on our phones. Instead of renting the P.A. equipment, using a livestream YouTube broadcast had been his idea. "It's like two mil in my pocket right off the top," Coupland explained. "And everyone knows how into this technology shit I am."

"Hi everyone," he modestly began. "I'm Doug."

"Hi Doug!" the crowd roared. Laughter boomed from all around us.

Coupland chuckled. "Tonight wouldn't be possible without the hard work and the research done by my friends at A.I. Plus Womxn's Health Solutions. By allowing me the privilege of seeing their beautiful science, they have enabled me to make Canada's largest living work of art. So Ray, Michael, Clara, Nick and Ravi, I want to thank you for leading the charge." More applause erupted all around us. Clara's eyes brimmed with happy tears.

"Behind the scenes, my dear friend Wu Chung, has been instrumental in building the infrastructure you are going to witness tonight. By creating the specimens you are about to see, and the infrastructure to manage them, Wu has created a practical solution to the threat of invasive Asian carp on our salmon fisheries, and our natural Pacific habitat."

The crowd thundered once again, and Mom put her arm around Wu's shoulders. "I'm very proud of you," she said.

"Thank you, Mother," Wu said.

Coupland continued. "The living art you are about to see serves a scientific purpose. The koi fish we are using not only drive invasive silver carp away from our fragile salmon fisheries, but they also produce a serum that is a breakthrough treatment in our fight against cancer."

More cheers came from all over. It felt like a stationary earthquake. The size of the spectacle made me tense. Clara led my hand to a synthetic fur-patch she's sewn along the side of her shirt. I began petting it, and felt instantly better.

"So, folks, the moment is upon us. I'll ask those of you near the water, if you could look in the base of the potted palms, you'll find a paper cup full of pellets. When you see the helicopters release their pellets, I'll ask you to do the same. And please, take a step back from the edge before you throw."

Three military Chinook helicopters, toting heavy slings, flew in low over the city and took position, hovering over

False Creek. A single bright orange firework exploded in the distance and the slings released, dropping thousands of pounds of fish food into the water. At the same time, those of us on the sidelines tossed handfuls of pellets from the shore.

False Creek boiled and frothed as millions of mutant koi started the largest feeding frenzy in known history. As this happened, the silver carp began flying hither and yon from the water, flipping and flopping to the shoreline, where they launched themselves into the potted palms. Tens of thousands of the despised silver fish ejected from the water as the surface turned brilliant, luminescent orange. False Creek, in the twilight, appeared to be ablaze.

Fireworks burst overhead – orange and yellow and white – and they added to the unprecedented spectacle.

Wu sidled up to Clara and me, his face a mask of concentration as he tossed handfuls of pellets.

"Wu," I said, "something's been bothering me."

"What is it, Nicholas?"

"What did you end up doing with Frances?"

He looked meaningfully at his fistful of pellets. "You know," he said, "these koi will eat just about anything."

**Jake Swan**

— A physician from Saint John, New Brunswick.
— Writes satire, and suffers from gastro-esophageal reflux.
— Worldview has been described as "Chaotic."
— Mother considers him "A disappointment."

www.ingramcontent.com/pod-product-compliance
Lightning Source LLC
Chambersburg PA
CBHW030858200726
48289CB00003B/801